. . . AND . . . CURTAIN!

"Who's this?" the actor playing Detective Carboroni asked the character Whittaker.

"My daughter's *former* suitor," Whittaker replied, sounding pleased.

"That you?" the detective said to Cynthia.

She responded by letting out a bloodcurdling wail and running from the stage. Her mother, Victoria, had collapsed on the couch, where she fanned herself with a magazine.

Carboroni nudged his toe into Paul's side. There was no response from the fallen actor.

It all sounded like scripted banter, but I sensed something was wrong. From my vantage point, I could tell that Paul hadn't moved a muscle since stumbling into the scene and falling at Cynthia's feet. The pool of fake blood had been widening. I saw a stricken look come over Larry Savoy's face. He motioned to Melinda in the wings, and the curtain began to close. . . .

A QUESTION OF MURDER

A *Murder, She Wrote* Mystery

A Novel by Jessica Fletcher
and Donald Bain
based on the
Universal television series
created by Peter S. Fischer,
Richard Levinson & William Link

A SIGNET BOOK

SIGNET
Published by New American Library, a division of
Penguin Group (USA) Inc., 375 Hudson Street,
New York, New York 10014, USA
Penguin Group (Canada), 90 Eglinton Avenue East, Suite 700, Toronto,
Ontario M4P 2Y3, Canada (a division of Pearson Penguin Canada Inc.)
Penguin Books Ltd., 80 Strand, London WC2R 0RL, England
Penguin Ireland, 25 St. Stephen's Green, Dublin 2,
Ireland (a division of Penguin Books Ltd.)
Penguin Group (Australia), 250 Camberwell Road, Camberwell, Victoria 3124,
Australia (a division of Pearson Australia Group Pty. Ltd.)
Penguin Books India Pvt. Ltd., 11 Community Centre, Panchsheel Park,
New Delhi - 110 017, India
Penguin Group (NZ), cnr Airborne and Rosedale Roads, Albany,
Auckland 1310, New Zealand (a division of Pearson New Zealand Ltd.)
Penguin Books (South Africa) (Pty.) Ltd., 24 Sturdee Avenue,
Rosebank, Johannesburg 2196, South Africa

Penguin Books Ltd., Registered Offices:
80 Strand, London WC2R 0RL, England

First published by Signet, an imprint of New American Library,
a division of Penguin Group (USA) Inc.

First Printing, April 2006
10 9 8 7 6 5 4 3 2 1

For good friends,
Denise Lee and Michael Millius

NOTE: The answers to the questions that appear at the beginning of each chapter can be found at the end of the book.

No peeking!

Chapter One

The girl was young and pretty. The large yellow sun-
flowers on the mid-calf-length white dress she wore
perfectly matched her blond hair and seemingly sunny
disposition. Her smile was wide and genuine; there
was a sweetness about her that was palpable.

The young man, named Paul, standing next to her
was not so sanguine. He was of medium height and
wore a brooding expression along with his khaki
slacks, two-tone boat shoes, and pale blue button-
down shirt. A maroon cardigan tied loosely around
his neck and draped down his back completed his
preppy wardrobe. He was handsome in a rough sort
of way. By that I mean there was a thickness to his
facial features that contributed to what seemed like
a perpetual frown. He lacked interest in the others
in the drawing room—with the single exception, of
course, of the young woman, whose name was
Cynthia.

With the young couple were an older man wearing

a purple silk smoking jacket, and a patrician woman in knee-high riding boots, wide-hipped tan jodhpurs, and a white silk blouse.

"Feel like taking a walk?" Paul asked Cynthia in a voice that carried to the others. Softly he added, "Let's get out of here." He ducked his head down, gave her a quick kiss on the neck, and stroked her arm, gliding his hand from her shoulder down to her fingers.

Cynthia shivered and took a step forward. "What a grand idea," she said, turning to the older couple. "I certainly could use a walk. I hear there's a full moon."

"You won't see any moon," declared the older man, whose name was Monroe Whittaker. "Not with the fog out there off the lake. Besides, there's still snow on the ground, and more in the forecast." His tone was that of a board chairman used to making statements that no one would dare challenge.

"That's okay, Daddy," Cynthia said, plucking at the collar of her dress. "It's so warm in here with the fire going. I really need some fresh air. I'm sure Paul does, too. Besides, you always say a walk after dinner is good for your digestion. Isn't that how you put it?"

His ruddy, full face set in stone, her father said nothing. Victoria Whittaker addressed Paul. "We have a very busy day tomorrow with the attorneys coming. Cynthia will need a clear head. I want to be sure she gets enough rest. Make sure you don't keep her out late again."

"He won't," Cynthia said, kissing her mother's cheek. They put on outdoor jackets, and she wrapped a red and green tartan scarf around her neck. Smiling at Paul, she grabbed his hand and led him through the French doors into the garden, her voice trailing back into the room. "Let's look for that moon anyway."

"I haven't changed my mind," Monroe Whittaker said the moment they were gone. "I don't like him."

"That's patently obvious," his wife said, checking her hair in the mirror over the fireplace. "But the least you can do is be civil to him this weekend."

"Civil?" Monroe snorted. "How about if I pack his bag and send him away from here? Would that be civil enough?"

"Monroe," his wife scolded, "you're not thinking clearly. Cynthia is like all young women her age. She's rebelling against us because it's the thing to do. I share your opinion of Paul. He's obviously not of Cynthia's class. I'll give him credit for trying to dress the part, although anyone can see the poor quality of his clothes." Her small laugh was dismissive. "Not that I'd expect him to know the difference. His father is a policeman in New York City. Good Lord, you know how crude policemen can be."

"A cop? How do you know that?"

Victoria turned to her husband, her hand still on her hair. "I don't recall exactly. Does it matter? He must have told me. But the point is that the more we challenge the young man, the more we'll push Cynthia into the relationship. Trust me, darling, the best way to see the last of him is to shower him with kindness and expose him to our daughter's lifestyle and breeding. He'll become uncomfortable soon enough and seek his own kind." She turned back to the mirror. "I think I'll go up. Are you coming?"

"Not yet," he growled.

With that, Victoria left her husband alone in the room.

Monroe went to the doors and peered outside. "Damn fog," he muttered. He walked to his desk and slumped heavily in the chair, eyes narrowed, mouth set in a harsh slash. Suddenly, he slammed his fist on the desktop. He reached into a desk drawer, withdrew a bulky envelope that he shoved into the pocket of his smoking jacket, and stormed out the doors into the garden.

As he left, a maid carrying a carpet sweeper entered the room through another door. She leaned the sweeper against the wall, pulled a cloth from her apron pocket, and proceeded to dust the furniture, moving from a table to the mantel to the desk. She ran her dustrag across the desk's broad mahogany top, then paused and bit her lip. Her eyes darted from the French doors back toward the door through which she'd entered the room. Gingerly, so as not to make a sound, she drew open one drawer after another. Each time, she dipped down and twisted her body to see into the back, and rummaged inside with her free hand.

Victoria's voice could be heard from another room. "Monroe, have you seen my handbag?"

The maid swiftly closed the drawers, ran to the other end of the room, and resumed her dusting. She was only a minute into her chores when the room's stillness was assaulted by the sound of a weapon being discharged somewhere outside, followed by a woman's piercing scream.

Cynthia burst through the doors. "Help!" she shouted. "Someone help me!"

Paul stumbled into the room behind her, his jacket open, his hand pressed against his chest. Cardinal red blood oozed through his fingers and ran down the front of his blue shirt. The maid gasped, covering her mouth with her hand. Then, wailing, she rushed out the door and was replaced by Monroe and Victoria Whittaker coming in from opposite ends of the room. Paul fell to his knees at Cynthia's feet. With a final, agonizing gasp, he pitched forward, his face coming to rest on her shoe.

"Daddy!" Cynthia shrieked and collapsed into her father's arms, sobbing.

Victoria tiptoed toward the prone body and leaned in closer. "Is he dead?" she asked calmly.

Her husband scowled down at the body on the floor and looked over at his wife. "Yes, I'd say he's dead. Very dead."

Chapter Two

In what Agatha Christie book did her Belgian detective, Hercule Poirot, make his first appearance?

Lawrence Savoy clapped his hands to gain everyone's attention. "Okay, folks, that wasn't bad. Let's try it one more time. And Paul, try to avoid Cynthia's shoe when you land on the floor. Makes it hard for her to fall into her daddy's arms if her foot is stuck under your head."

"Yeah, yeah," Paul said, as he removed his shirt and handed it to the props girl. "What a mess! Laura, you put too much blood in the sponge."

"It'll wash out," Savoy said. "At least we know the prop works. The blood came right through your fingers just the way we wanted it to. We'll do it without the blood this time. Just be aware of Cynthia's foot." Savoy took a few steps away, stopped, turned, and added, "And Paul, project, please. This isn't a scene from a movie. Your Brando mumble doesn't work on the stage. It's a play with a live audience. P-r-o-j-e-c-t!"

"Yeah, Larry, okay," Paul said, shrugging on the fresh shirt Laura held out for him. He grabbed the towel she'd slung over her shoulder and wiped his hands.

"It's Mr. Savoy," the director chided, crossing the stage to where Paul stood. "My friends call me Larry, but you haven't achieved that status. Just because you come from a theatrical family and were in some B movies doesn't impress me."

Paul smirked, tossed the towel back at the props girl, and sat next to Cynthia on the sofa.

"Victoria, my darling," Savoy called from where he'd taken a seat in the fourth row of the auditorium. "You found just the right arrogance, my sweet, but I want to see a little more evasiveness when Monroe asks you about Paul's father. And Monroe, please can that British accent. We're supposed to be in Connecticut, not the Cotswolds."

"I can't help the way I speak, Lawrence," Monroe said.

"Of course you can. You're an actor. Just put on a Connecticut accent."

"And what, precisely, is a Connecticut accent?"

Savoy closed his eyes and slowly shook his head. He looked up again and said, "Just tone it down. Okay?"

Cynthia put her hands against Paul's chest and shoved him against the arm of the sofa. She popped up from her seat and stormed to the edge of the stage. "Mr. Savoy," she said, her face suffused with anger, "will you please tell him to stop mauling me? If he can't keep his hands to himself, I swear I'll sock him, even if we're in the middle of a scene."

"Really, young man," Monroe said, scowling at the young actor. "How unprofessional."

"Hardly surprising," Victoria added.

Paul grinned, ran a hand through his dark hair, and retied the sleeves of the maroon sweater around his neck. He eyed his older colleagues and shrugged. "Some of us still have urges," he said. "Besides, she's just so beautiful, I can't help myself." He winked at Cynthia, who stamped her foot in frustration.

"Well, learn some control," Savoy said, "or you're out. There are dozens of actors in New York who would jump at an opportunity like this. I won't have someone polarizing the cast."

Paul raised his palms in mock submission. " 'Polarizing?' I'm as bad as that, huh? Okay, okay, I promise I'll be good."

"I'll assume you mean that," Savoy said, picking up a clipboard and making notes. "Now, places everyone. We're in Act One, Scene Two."

Cynthia flopped down next to Paul, struggling to keep her expression neutral. Monroe Whittaker took his place across from Victoria and the actors played the scene again.

"It looks like it's going very well," I whispered to Melinda Savoy, Lawrence's wife. We were watching a rehearsal for the play that would form the centerpiece of the murder mystery weekend taking place at Mohawk House, a rustic, sprawling lakeside lodge in the foothills of the Berkshires. I had been invited to be on a panel of mystery writers, an extra entertainment to complement the mystery performed by the Savoys' theatrical troupe.

"Larry added the line about the fog and snow today to make it more realistic," Melinda said. "He likes to do that so the audience feels like it's actually happening." She waved an arm toward the windows, the view from which was obscured by a heavy white mist. "Look at that. You can't even see your hand in front of you." She extended her arm and squinted at her fingers as if the fog were obscuring her view.

"That always happens when the weather warms up quickly before the snow has had a chance to melt," I said. "I can't believe the forecast for later today. A blizzard!"

"Maybe they're wrong," Melinda said.

"Let's hope so."

The weather in the Berkshires had been inordinately warm for early March, the "lamb" part of the month coming in before the "lion" had a chance to roar, although winter wasn't finished yet. Typical of March, one minute it was sunny and mild, the next windy and cold. From the forecasts I'd seen on TV and read in the newspapers, a freak snowstorm was due to hit within hours and could dump as much as three feet of heavy, wet white stuff.

I had to smile at the contribution the fog coming off the lake was making to our interactive murder mystery weekend. Nothing like a pea-souper to enhance a sense of dread and foul things to come. In large-scale theatrical productions and high-budget motion pictures, they use expensive machines to create fog. Here we were enjoying it without it costing a cent, thanks to our special-effects director, Mother Nature.

The Savoys were adept at taking advantage of the built-in atmosphere. I was familiar with their methods, having made appearances at other events at which they had provided the entertainment. They took their shows all over the globe, performing at corporate gatherings and society fund-raisers, aboard luxury cruise ships, and, of course, at myriad weekends such as this one at Mohawk House. When Melinda Savoy had called to say she'd recommended me and the marketing department wanted me to join the authors' panel, I'd been happy to accept.

"A character will get killed during the play, Jessica," she said brightly. "Nothing you aren't accustomed to."

"Try not to make it during dinner," I replied. "You don't want to spoil the guests' appetites."

"Nor mine. The dining room is off-limits, I assure you. The only dead people at Mohawk House will be onstage. Speaking of off-limits: Don't let anyone rope you into helping them solve the crime." She laughed. "I have enough trouble coming up with these complicated scenarios without having to worry that an expert will expose my plot after the first act."

"Of course," I said, laughing along with her. "But your plays are wonderful. I'm sure I'll be just as mystified as the rest of the audience. It sounds as though you're in the midst of a busy season."

"Insanely busy. The play we're doing this weekend is a new one, which always has its share of problems until the kinks get ironed out. We've got two dozen appearances booked over the next three months. That's good for our bottom line and for the actors, but it has us running in circles," she said with a chuckle. "But that's our problem, not yours. I'm so pleased you'll join us. It'll be fun, I promise."

So there I was, in the rolling hills of Connecticut at a historic mansion that dated back almost two hundred years. It had been a resort for the past fifty. As the story went, its original owner—the third son of a British earl, well out of line to inherit his father's lands and title—had built an elaborate log cabin as a kind of architectural tribute to his new country. Subsequent occupants, however, enamored with the building's aristocratic lineage, had added on their visions of what a noble house ought to look like until the resulting hodgepodge was a frightening, albeit fascinating, mix of Tudor, Georgian, and Adirondack styles with a few medieval details thrown in.

The architecture wasn't the only fascinating thing about Mohawk House, however. It came replete with its own ghost story to tickle the imaginations of its guests. According to legend, this same third son of a British earl was brutally murdered one night as he slept in the master bedroom suite. His head was severed and left on the pillow but his body was nowhere to be found, nor was the murder weapon. It was assumed that the murderer had weighted down the earl's decapitated body and taken it out into the middle of the glacial lake, hundreds of feet deep, and dumped it there to be entombed in the frigid black water for eternity.

According to what I'd read in Mohawk House's promotional literature, there were a number of suspects, none of whom ever confessed to the crime, nor were any of them charged. The mystery gave rise to some tall tales. It was said in the days and weeks following the murder that by severing the head from the body, the killer had enabled the earl's soul to escape and live on in the house. There had been countless reports of "sightings" of the murder victim at odd hours of the night, dressed in a crimson satin robe and red satin slippers with turned-up toes, and carrying a large curved axe with a bloody blade, presumably the weapon used to slay him. Scary stuff if you believed in such tales, all good fun if you didn't.

"I think I'm due for a good walk before the others arrive," I said.

"Your author colleagues?" said Melinda. "They're already here. Mark Egmon from the hotel arrived with them in tow and introduced them to us. They left just minutes before you walked in."

"I'm sorry I missed them," I said. "I'll just have to wait for dinner to meet them. Actually, I know John Chasseur."

Melinda's eyebrows went up. "Quite the Romeo, isn't he? Or aspires to be."

"I don't know him that well, Melinda. We've been on a few author panels together in the past, nothing more than that. I'm looking forward to meeting GSB Wick. I really admire her books."

"Nice lady. She's so tiny, like a little bird. I love her Southern drawl." Melinda giggled.

"What's funny?"

"Paul, the actor who plays Cynthia's suitor, started flirting with Ms. Wick. He's always flirting with someone. I think she was annoyed. She was with a friend, an elderly British gentleman, she brought for the weekend." She leaned close. "Larry's upset that I hired Paul to play the part of the suitor. Larry says he's nothing but trouble, but he's good. He plays the part beautifully."

I was about to leave to go on my walk when Lawrence Savoy suddenly got up and asked, "Who are those people up on the stage?"

A dozen men and women, presumably paying guests, had wandered onto the set through a side door leading to the stage.

"Excuse me," Savoy said.

A young woman carrying a clipboard came to the stage apron. "I told them we were in rehearsal, but they just—"

"It's okay," said Savoy. To the guests he said, "I'm sorry, folks, but this is a closed rehearsal."

"We just wanted to see what was going on," said an older woman who was with a man I assumed was her husband. They wore matching argyle sweaters, his a vest, hers a cardigan.

The husband spoke: "We were told guests are

encouraged to make themselves at home and explore the hotel."

"Okay," Savoy said, "but I'm afraid that doesn't include rehearsals. Besides, you don't want to ruin the surprise before you see the play."

"We're looking for clues," her husband said with a mischievous smile.

Savoy laughed. "You'll have to look for them somewhere else."

The woman smiled sweetly and said, "Of course." To her husband, "Come, dear." She led him away, with the others falling in behind.

"Always something," Melinda said.

"All right," Savoy said to the cast. "Places!"

He'd no sooner returned to his seat when a loud crash came from somewhere offstage.

"What was that?" he bellowed.

A strapping young man wearing a T-shirt and jeans and carrying a hammer joined the cast. He peered out into the house, spotted Savoy, and said, "I can't fit the set through the door."

"Oh, that's great," Savoy said, "just great." He returned to the stage. "Can't you take it apart and put it back together once you've got it in place?" he asked the young man.

"Not easily," came the response.

"That's Jeremy," Melinda told me. "He's our lead stagehand."

"Easy or not," said Savoy, "you have to get it in here. Do whatever you have to, but do it quick. We're running late."

"Right," Jeremy said, not sounding pleased. He shouted to the others, "Hey, anybody see my pick?"

"Pick?" I said to Melinda.

"One of a stagehand's basic tools, like gaffer tape. You know, duct tape. Crew use picks to temporarily hold things down on the set."

"Jeremy," Savoy said loudly, "please. Not now. Your pick will show up."

"I know I laid it down back here," said Jeremy, wandering off the stage.

Melinda left my side to confer with her husband, which gave me the opportunity to slip out and embark on that walk I'd been looking forward to. I was glad to get away. I'd become uncomfortable with the tension in the room even though I'd been around enough theatrical productions to know that nerves often frayed and tempers rose when talented, creative performers act out their frustrations—as well as their roles.

I trekked out to the lakeshore, where I stood and looked back at the forbidding structure of Mohawk House. It was shrouded in mist, its stone-clad turrets visible when the fog would suddenly part, only to be obscured moments later when the haze swirled around them again.

I shivered. Despite the premature warming, it had turned damp and chilly, and I could "smell" snow in the air. If the weather forcasters were correct, we were in for a doozy of a spring snowstorm. Although I'd put on what I thought would be warm enough clothing, I wished I'd added an extra layer before head-

ing outside. I put into play some positive thinking—
The exercise will warm me up, I assured myself—and
turned away from the building as I rubbed my
arms briskly.

But I never did get warm. The expedition was
short-lived. I hadn't been gone more than ten minutes before it became apparent that I wasn't going to
get very far along the trail. My intention had been
to walk around the lake, but those best-laid plans
were thwarted by the vapors, which thickened and
rose from the surface of the glacial pool, rolling over
the land and filling the valley. They enveloped me,
slowing my steps and making the scenic hike along
the rocky, icy track too risky to continue.

Wrapped in the mist, I became disoriented. Had I
wandered off the path? Was I too close to the lake?
The sharp sound of cracking ice fired off to my right.
Oh dear, I thought. One errant move and I could tum-
ble off a ledge and down into the frigid waters. I
remembered reading about mountain climbers getting caught in a "whiteout" when the snow swirled
so heavily around them that they couldn't tell which
direction they'd been heading, or even distinguish
up from down. Imitating Melinda's motion earlier, I
stuck out my arm. I could see my hand, but not
much else in front of me. There were some shadows
that might be tall trees. The weight of the air made
breathing difficult. My walking shoes sank into the
damp earth and little puddles filled my footprints.
Looks like an early mud season, I told myself, trying to

get my bearings. Back home in Cabot Cove, Maine, "mud season" is what we call the long melt between winter's frost and the appearance of the first blades of grass in the spring.

As I felt a few snowflakes on my cheeks, the thought of a roaring fire in my suite compelled me. I carefully retraced my steps down the path in the direction of the hotel. I began to shiver, not quite sure if it was the cold or the apprehension of taking a wrong step that set off the tremors. The mist lifted slightly as I retraced my steps across a rickety wooden walkway with rope railings, and I sighed heavily in relief when I reached a back entrance to the building. I paused just outside the door. I could hear muffled voices, male and female, on the other side.

"If you think you're going to get away with this, you have another think coming."

"Stop being so melodramatic."

"You can dismiss this, but I'll have the last laugh."

"Yeah? What are you going to do? Kill me?"

I thought I heard a scuffle. I turned the doorknob. The heavy door squealed when I opened it and the sound of someone hurrying up the stairs echoed in the hall. I stepped inside, my eyes not yet acclimated to the gloom, and came face-to-face with the young actor who played Paul in the production. A cigarette in his hand, he stood alone, partially hidden by shadows that engulfed most of the concrete area just inside the door. A single low-wattage bulb in a wall sconce shaped like a torch cast uncertain light, but it was enough for me to see the gleam of sweat on his brow and the look of fury on his face.

"My goodness," I said. "You startled me."

"Sorry," he said sullenly.

I looked at where he was standing. Judging from the half dozen cigarette butts scattered on the floor, this small alcove was where smokers retreated when the urge struck them. There was a no-smoking policy throughout the resort, which had no guest rooms for smokers. It occurred to me that the management of Mohawk House, knowing smokers came here to indulge, would have been smart to provide an urn or other receptacle in which they could extinguish their cigarettes.

"No need to apologize," I said. "You didn't do anything except stand here. I simply wasn't expecting anyone. I was just out for a walk, but the weather made it impossible." I hugged myself and rubbed the backs of my arms. "Brrrr," I said. "It's chilly out there, and the snow has started. The dampness goes right through you. The fog—"

He pushed away from the wall, crushing the half-consumed cigarette beneath the heel of his shoe, and took the narrow, winding concrete steps two at a time.

Well, I must say I've had more pleasant encounters, I thought ruefully. *It seems the climate inside is no better than it is outside.*

Chapter Three

*Which mystery writer features cats and dogs
in her novels?*

Don't take offense, I told myself. *He's an actor. He's probably absorbed in his role, preparing for tonight's performance.
Maybe it's the fog and the threat of snow, bringing out
the worst in people, making them feel claustrophobic and
trapped.*

I shrugged my shoulders to release the tension,
and to dismiss the uneasy feeling I'd begun to develop about Mohawk House and the weekend. I
glanced about the smokers' vestibule, my eyes now
used to the dim light. Had I had a dustpan and
broom, I would have tidied up—my New England
neatness genes coming to the fore. Instead, I as-
cended the staircase Paul had used to escape my
presence and stepped into the warmth of the main
hallway.

At one end of the hallway was the lobby, where
an inglenook welcomed guests in from the cold. A
pair of benches flanked the blazing fire and drew
some of those who were waiting to register for the
long weekend. Once they signed in, they were

directed to a table where team assignments were
handed out along with a packet of written materials.
The teams would compete with each other to solve
the "murder" that would take place during the
course of the festivities, staged as part of the play,
of course. Unless guests traveled to Mohawk House
together and had requested that they be on the same
team of amateur sleuths, they were paired with others on a random basis to ensure equality in numbers.

The other end of the long hallway in which I stood
terminated in the dining area of the old building. I
knew from experience that certain cast members
would mingle at the tables and pretend to be guests,
their true identity revealed only later in the play. The
actors and actresses cast by the Savoys were amazingly adroit at concealing their true identities, and
I'd marveled on more than one occasion at their
skills, not only at playing their scripted roles in the
show, but also at slipping into other, offstage perso-
nas. The guests were in for a weekend of fun, which
I was sure would include more than one surprise.

"Mrs. Fletcher?"

I turned to see Mark Egmon approaching. Mark
was Mohawk House's manager of special events and
theme programs, including the annual mystery
weekends.

"So glad I found you," he said. "All settled in
your room?"

"Oh, yes," I said. "It's lovely. I especially appreciate the fireplace and the balcony. What a lovely
view."

"I'm so glad you like it. It's one of my favorite rooms."

"I imagine there are many wonderful rooms here."

"They're all nice. That's the official line," he said with a wink and a smile. "But yours is part of the original structure and has some surprising features. I'm not going to tell you what they are. You'll just have to discover them yourself."

"That sounds intriguing."

"Have you seen your books in our shop? Let me show you. The store manager has a nice touch. She used to be a window decorator."

He escorted me to a table in the gift store where my books, and those of the other authors in attendance, had been artfully arranged.

"What a nice display," I said, picking up John Chasseur's latest thriller. "I bought this book last week," I said, noting his signature on the title page. "Will you be having a book signing?"

"Yes, but we are suggesting that the authors autograph some of their books in advance. If you have time, you can do it right now. Some guests will want to skip the author panel and book signing, but buy signed books anyway. Would you mind?"

"Of course not."

He brought me a chair and hovered solicitously while I wrote the date, a greeting, and my name in two dozen copies of my new mystery. As I finished each one, the shop manager affixed a sticker on the book that said SIGNED BY AUTHOR and replaced it in the pile on the table.

"That's something else I can check off my list," Mark said, walking me out of the shop. "Thank you so much." At the door, his expression turned regretful. "Listen, I hate to put you on the spot," he said, "but I was wondering whether you've had a chance to come up with your first question."

"As a matter of fact, I have it right here," I said, reaching into my pocket and extracting a slip of paper. "I have the others in my room."

He adjusted half-glasses and read the question I had written down.

"Perfect," he said. "Nothing like Dame Agatha to get things rolling. I have to run now. See you at dinner."

I watched him bound down the hallway and smiled, satisfied that he'd been pleased at the question I'd come up with. When I accepted the invitation to be on the writers' panel, I was told that each panelist was expected to come up with a series of questions that would be presented to the guests over the course of the weekend. Lawrence Savoy would read the questions before the start of each performance, and the audience members were to write their answers on a card provided in their packets of written materials. The person with the most correct answers would receive a free weekend at the resort. The cards would be collected at each performance to avoid having someone retreat to his or her room and consult a book or go on the Internet.

I'd agonized over the questions before leaving Cabot Cove. Aware that there would be many knowledgeable mystery lovers in the audience, I didn't want my questions to be overly simplistic. At the same time, I wanted to avoid getting too esoteric for those whose knowledge was marginal. My instructions were to start with a relatively easy question and make each one progressively harder. The one I'd given Mark Egmon had to do with the first appearance of Agatha Christie's Belgian detective, Hercule Poirot. Simple enough, I thought, for Christie devotees, but perhaps not so easy for less widely read mystery fans.

My thoughts about the question were interrupted by the sound of an altercation in the lobby. Angry words carried above the general drone of people talking. They drew me down the hall, where I witnessed what was happening. A middle-aged woman standing in the registration line shouted at a tall, redheaded woman dressed all in black, including a black lace veil. "Go to the back of the line. You can't just cut in front of me."

"I beg your pardon. I did not cut in. A lady wouldn't do such a thing, and I am above all a lady," the redhead retorted in the raspy, high-pitched voice often associated with heavy smokers. She towered over the other woman.

"You did cut in on us," a man, presumably the other woman's husband, told the redhead. Short and round, with his fists resting on his hips, he reminded me of a little teapot as he glared up into her face.

The redhead looked down at the couple. "If I offended you," she said, "I certainly didn't intend to.

But I suggest that you temper your—temper." She giggled and flounced away, looking back and wiggling her fingers at the couple.

I hope they don't end up on the same team, I thought as I ambled down the hall to the elevators and pushed the UP button. The elevator arrived and I entered the empty car. The doors were nearly closed when an arm, draped in black, was thrust through the narrow opening.

"Good heavens," I said, darting forward, searching the panel for the DOOR OPEN button, but the arm had accomplished the same task. "I'm sorry," I said, as the door slid back to reveal the redheaded woman. "I didn't see you coming or I would have held it."

"That's all right, dearie," she said, peering at me from under the veil. She whirled around to face the door, her ankle-length black skirt following her. Her arm shot out and I saw the button for the third floor light up.

With her back to me, her face was concealed, but I couldn't help but smile. She was probably one of Melinda Savoy's creations. Melinda reveled in throwing mysterious characters into the mix, characters who might never appear onstage but who would capture the attention of the guests and be linked to the solution in the end, most likely in improbable ways. You never really knew who was real and who wasn't until the end of the weekend.

I exited the elevator at my floor and entered my room. I was delighted to find that someone from housekeeping had considerately put a match to the

logs in the fireplace to take the chill out of the air. I
picked up the John Chasseur novel I'd brought with
me, kicked off my shoes, and drew a chair up in
front of the grate, resting my heels on an embroi-
dered footstool. The heat was relaxing, and several
pages into the book I became drowsy and nodded
off, my chin dropping against my breastbone. Then
an icy draft nipped my neck. I came awake with a
start, the book sliding off my lap and landing on the
floor. This wouldn't do, I realized. Dinner was within
the hour, with a welcoming speech and the first act
of the play to take place after dinner in the massive
auditorium where I'd seen that afternoon's rehearsal.
A quick wake-up shower was in order.

I changed into a terry-cloth robe provided by the
hotel and spent a few minutes standing under water
that threatened to become hot but never quite did,
although it was warm enough for its purpose. Re-
freshed, I stepped back into the bedroom. The wind
had picked up outside, sending currents of cold air
through unseen cracks around the windows and the
French doors leading to the balcony. I went to the
doors, over which I'd drawn heavy gray drapes, with
the intention of pulling them even tighter against the
drafts. A loud crash from the balcony caused me to
tense and take a few steps back. What could that
have been?

I tightened the belt on the robe, opened the drapes
slightly, and peered into the gloom. The light fixture
just outside the door casing revealed nothing except
blowing snow. The storm had started. I pulled aside

the drapes and opened one of the doors. The source of the noise was now evident. The wind had blown a glass container of some sort from a railing to the cement floor of the balcony. Despite the cold and the swirling snow—the temperature had dropped considerably over the past hour—I stepped outside and leaned over to examine the mess. It must have been a large ashtray because an assortment of half-consumed cigarettes lay on the floor along with the broken glass. I noted that a few of the cigarettes had lipstick on the filters. Obviously, whoever had previously occupied the room had used the balcony to indulge their habit. Probably a couple, I surmised, judging from the two different brands of cigarettes and the traces of lipstick on some of the cigarette butts.

I found a piece of cardboard in the closet and, leaving the balcony door ajar, went outside again to scoop up the glass and butts, with the intention of depositing them in a wastebasket in the room. But as I bent to my task, a gust of wind blew up and the door to my room slammed shut behind me with a bang. I gathered what was left of the glass ashtray and consumed cigarettes, and then, balancing the shards on the cardboard, I turned the knob on the door and pushed. The balcony door would not open.

Oh, for heaven's sakes, I thought. *Did it lock behind me?*

I set the cardboard down on a metal chair and tried the door again. It was stuck. When Mark Egmon said the room had *surprising* features, I didn't think this was what he had in mind. I rattled the doorknob, thinking perhaps it required a special touch. I have a few doors like that at home. Changes in the weather make them stick, and old latches sometimes temporarily freeze, usually when I'm in a hurry. And I was in a hurry now.

The terry robe, which had felt so cozy when I'd stepped out of the shower, was not much protection against the elements. I gathered the material close with one hand and tried the knob again. It turned freely, but the latch wouldn't budge. I pressed my hip against the door and twisted the knob again. It came off in my hand. I tried to put it back on, delicately probing for the rod to which the knob had been attached. My efforts were rewarded with the sound of a thud, and I looked in to see that the inside doorknob had fallen to the carpeted floor.

"Oh dear," I said aloud. I leaned out over the edge of the balcony, peering into the dark, hoping to see the windows of another room and perhaps catch the attention of its occupants. But there were no other windows in view. My room was in a corner of the building that thrust out over the lakeshore, which must provide a lovely daytime view when the weather was clear. I looked up. Perhaps someone was in the room above mine.

"Hello?" I called out. "Can anyone hear me? Hello? Is anyone there?"

My only answer was the sting of snow on my face, the wind curling around me, rushing through my hair, pulling at my robe, and rattling the panes of the door. *If worse comes to worst*, I thought, *I'll use one of the chairs to break the glass in the door.* I envisioned Mark Egmon's expression when I tried to explain why I had to destroy the room's beautiful French doors. I gave an involuntary shiver, and my teeth began to chatter. *I'd better figure this out quickly*, I thought, *before hypothermia sets in.* I imagined the headlines if I were unsuccessful. JESSICA FLETCHER FREEZES TO DEATH. MYSTERY WRITER COULDN'T SOLVE THE RIDDLE OF THE LOCK.

Next to the French doors was a window. It was an old-fashioned double-hung window, thank goodness, but the sill was very high, and my fingers couldn't get a grip on the wooden frame. I moved the cardboard and broken glass to the balcony floor, pulled the metal chair over to the window, and climbed onto the seat. Reaching up to where the bottom portion of the window ended, I pressed the heels of my palms into the frame and pushed. The window squealed in response, almost as if it objected to being handled roughly. But to my great relief, it moved. I managed to open a small gap, enough to fit my fingers through, and still standing on the chair, I pulled the window the rest of the way open. I passed the cardboard with the butts and shards of glass into the room and followed. Fortunately, no one could see me clamber through the open window while trying to keep the robe from flying off in the wind—it did claim one of my slippers—only to do battle with the heavy drapes on the inside before I emerged, unkempt but unscathed.

There wasn't time for a second shower. I washed

my hands and face and brushed my hair. Dressed for the evening, I checked myself in a full-length mirror on the back of the bathroom door and headed for a wide, carpeted staircase in the hallway. I would stop at the front desk later to report the broken knob on the French door.

As I turned a corner, the tall redhead I'd seen earlier came from the opposite direction, walking quickly. Even though her eyes were trained on the floor, I could see she was wearing heavy makeup under the dotted veil attached to a black hat that matched her dress. Her attention diverted, she almost bumped into me.

"My, my," she said, "we meet again. Clumsy old me." She carried on in the direction she'd been going before we almost collided.

Quite a character, I thought as I continued toward the staircase. It would be interesting to see what role she played in the production. I reached the top and started down. Halfway down the steps, the heel of my right shoe caught in a frayed portion of the carpeting, causing me to stumble. I grabbed the brass railing for support and managed to right myself, suffering only embarrassment at my clumsiness in front of the same white-haired couple with matching sweaters I'd seen on the stage a few hours earlier. They gave one another a swift glance as they passed me on the stairs, their eyes averted. I was baffled by their aloof behavior—they did not even pause to inquire if I was all right. Then it dawned on me. *They must think I'm tipsy.*

All in all, I thought as I reached the bottom of the stairs, straightened my skirt, and walked into the dining room, *this evening is not getting off to an auspicious start.*

Chapter Four

The origin of the detective story is generally attributed to what nineteenth-century writer?

Mohawk House's dining room was cavernous. Whoever had decided fifty years ago to convert the structure into a resort had turned the ballroom into a restaurant. The ceiling was easily thirty feet high, and was decorated with painted scenes that the artist evidently considered examples of classic European art. I would have to disagree.

The paint had faded badly, and small patches from some of the scenes had disengaged from the ceiling over the years, leaving gaps in the images. Huge, ornate chandeliers formed a line along the center of the ceiling; they were augmented by more modern lighting from wall sconces and strategically installed recessed fixtures. Large tapestries, some of them showing their age, provided the primary wall decorations and blocked drafts from ill-fitting windows. Between them were large framed portraits of turn-of-the-century men and women, perhaps those who'd actually lived in the mansion during that period.

A young hostess ushered me to a round table by

a window that I knew overlooked the lake, although the fog and snow precluded any enjoyment of it that evening. Already seated were the other writers I'd be joining on the panel.

John Chasseur was more youthful in appearance than the last time I'd seen him. I knew he was a regular visitor to his plastic surgeon's office—he'd once presented me with his doctor's card, "just in case."

"Good to see you again, Jessica," he said, rising.

The stunning blonde with him, whom Chasseur introduced as his wife, Claudette, appeared to be half his age. She gave me what amounted to a smile as she took my hand without comment.

"You're looking well," I told Chasseur.

"It's the Hollywood glow," he replied. "We bought a place in Malibu and I'm swimming every day. It sure beats this dreadful weather. A blizzard in March. You can have it."

His bronzed face looked more like a tanning-parlor tan to me, but I didn't say so.

"Do you know GSB Wick?" Chausseur asked, indicating the second woman at the table.

"We haven't had the pleasure before," I said, smiling and extending my hand. "I'm a great admirer of your work."

"You thought I was older, right?" she said. "Everyone does."

The warm tone of her Louisiana accent contrasted with her severe appearance. GSB Wick, whose storytelling style had led me to expect an older woman, was far younger than I. I'd already read her bio, in the conference brochure, though, so I now knew she was forty-four. She was a striking woman who didn't look her age. Her face was the palest white, her hair inky black and shaped tightly about her head like a helmet. She wore crimson lipstick and green eye shadow with tiny sparkles in it. I noticed how thin she was under the black dress she wore; her pale arms extended from half sleeves like matchsticks. Her books dealt with the supernatural, New Orleans voodoo, the deceased rising from their crypts, and vampires stalking the innocent in the wee hours on the streets of the French Quarter. When reading her works, I was taken with her ability to weave such subject matter into stories that were distinctly contemporary, featuring modern detectives fully grounded in the here and now. Applying the term "artistic" to her was not exaggeration.

Sitting next to her was a portly, elderly, ruddy-faced gentleman dressed in a vested brown tweed suit.

"This is a friend of mine, Harold Boynton," she said. "He's visiting from London."

"Terribly pleased to meet you, Mrs. Fletcher," he said, taking my outstretched hand and caressing it.

I took my seat just as Lawrence and Melinda Savoy joined us.

"I believe I've read just about everything you've written, Jessica," GSB Wick said as menus were placed before us. "You're among my favorites."

"I'm flattered to hear that," I said. "Your books

occupy an honored place on my bookshelves back home in Cabot Cove." I didn't add that, like many of her fans, I wondered what her initials stood for. In interviews, she had steadfastly refused to reveal her full name, a public relations stunt that had served her well. The Internet was full of sites devoted to speculation about her initials and the names they represented. I wasn't even sure if her publisher knew. I'd heard rumors, but none were based upon tangible knowledge.

"Georgie's newest book is doing splendidly," her British companion said.

Well, there's one part revealed—G for Georgie. What was that a nickname for? Georgia, perhaps, or Georgina. Maybe by the time the weekend was over, I'd learn what the S and B represented. I decided not to wait.

"Why do you use initials?" I asked.

Georgie sat back and sighed before responding, "When I started writing, I didn't want anyone to know whether my books were written by a man or a woman. Using initials accomplished that. Your by-line is J. B. Fletcher. For the same purpose, Jessica?"

"Partially," I said. "I know that when Phyllis James started her wonderful writing career in England, she was concerned that there would be a bias against female mystery writers, and so she became P. D. James. Whether there was or not—bias, that is—I don't know. In my case, the publisher thought my name was too long to fit with the type size he wanted to use on the cover. I didn't want to use a pseudonym, so we compromised. I've always liked the neutrality of initials, however. People tend to come to the books with different expectations."

"Exactly," she said.

"If there was a bias against women, I'm sure there was a good reason for it," Chasseur said. While everyone else at the table had dressed for dinner, Chasseur wore a white T-shirt with a picture of the cover of his latest novel emblazoned on the chest. Jeans, sandals, and white socks completed the outfit.

"What good reason could there possibly be, sir?" Georgie asked, taking the bait.

Chasseur smiled, revealing very white teeth that were slightly too large for his mouth. "I don't think women handle violent crime, particularly murder, as well as men do," he said, sitting back, obviously pleased with his analysis.

Georgie looked at me and rolled her eyes.

"That's an interesting theory," I said, "but I'm sure you'll excuse me for disagreeing."

Chasseur said, "Murder is a grisly, nasty business, Jessica. The female species simply doesn't have the genetic makeup to deal sensibly with it. Murder is a cold-blooded act. Women are, by nature, warmer-blooded than men, which is why they're so attractive to the male of the species."

"I think you're just teasing us, Mr. Chasseur," Georgie said, her Southern accent thickening. "And Ah'm not going let you pull my chain."

"John loves to drop bombs and see who comes running," his wife said in a bored voice.

"Claudette, my sweet," Chasseur said, his smile more a grimace now, "you're supposed to sit here and look pretty. It's not your intellectual insight we're interested in."

"It's not anything of mine you're interested in," she replied, her eyes flashing momentarily before resuming their vacant expression.

I realized that pursuing the debate over gender advantage in mystery writing would not accomplish anything other than to create more tension at the table, so I made a conscious decision to drop the subject.

Melinda Savoy also must have sensed the awkwardness of the moment, because she jumped in with, "This might be a good time to go over the schedule with you. But maybe we should order first."

Once our drink and appetizer orders had been placed, Melinda explained what our roles would be for the weekend. "There is, of course, the author panel," she said. "I'll moderate, but I'm sure I won't have to say much. My three guest authors have plenty of tales to tell to keep the audience interested."

"How long will we have to speak?" Georgie asked.

"The session's scheduled for an hour and a half. Other than the panel, you're pretty much free until the final day, when you'll judge the competition."

"Competition?" Chasseur asked.

"The guests have been broken up into teams," Lawrence Savoy said. "They'll follow the action all weekend and put their heads together to solve the murder mystery we present in the play. We encourage them to present their conclusions in some sort of skit—singing, costumes, whatever creative approaches they come up with. You'll decide which ones make the most entertaining presentations and come closest to solving the mystery. The winning team will choose one of its members to enjoy a free weekend at Mohawk House."

Melinda added, "What's really important is that you make yourselves available to the guests throughout the weekend. They're here because they love the murder mystery genre, and they're looking forward to socializing with famous writers."

"I'm not good at small talk," Chasseur said, sounding irritated. "It bores me."

"Everything bores you," I heard his wife mutter, although I would have thought she was the bored party in their marriage.

"You'll do just fine," I said, not sure why I felt compelled to allay his concerns. "They just want to know about you and your characters, subjects on which you're an expert."

Our waitress, a pert and pretty young woman who'd introduced herself as Jody, had the bountiful energy and ready smile of a college coed, which it turned out she was. Clearly thrilled that she'd been assigned "the authors," she responded enthusiastically when Chasseur engaged her in conversation that was overtly flirtatious. I glanced at Claudette, whose sour expression said her husband's behavior wasn't lost on her, and I had the impression that it was nothing she hadn't seen before.

GSB Wick was served the Bacardi cocktail she'd ordered. Her companion, Harold, was on his second martini, each sip raising the ruddiness of his cheeks and nose.

"What a beautiful color," I said, admiring the shimmering green liquid in Ms. Wick's large cocktail glass.

"A daiquiri with a teaspoon of grenadine instead of sugar," she said, tasting the drink. She nodded her approval and downed half of it in a single swallow.

I took a sip of my iced tea and responded to what the Savoys had said was expected of us. "I enjoy meeting mystery fans," I said, "and look forward to talking with them. That's what I like about lecturing and book tours. I actually get to meet the people who are reading what I've written."

"The way I see it," said Chasseur, obviously recovered from his momentary insecurity, "the great unwashed reading public suffers from a terminal case of hero worship, and who am I not to indulge them?" He called out to Jody in a loud voice, "Another martini, sweetheart, dryer this time. Tell the bartender to put a little vermouth in the air-conditioning."

Boynton laughed heartily. "Jolly good line," he said to Chasseur, his words slightly slurred. "I must remember it."

"Harold isn't a writer," Georgie said of her friend, "but he collects one-liners."

"Always enjoy a good turn of phrase," he said.

The Savoys were called away from the table several times to take care of last-minute production details and answer questions brought to them by cast members. They finally gave up on the idea of having dinner with us and disappeared from the room.

There was little anxiety during the rest of dinner, although Chasseur's occasional suggestive comments to Jody caused some discomfort—but apparently not for his wife, who ignored him.

Claudette was an interesting woman. She was beautiful. No one would debate that. She had the classic American looks seen in every fashion magazine: straight blond hair, golden tan skin, wide blue eyes, full lips under a delicate nose. She would draw attention—especially male attention—wherever she went, but I doubted she would reciprocate. Her manner seemed aloof and disdainful. It would have been easy to assume she possessed a vapid personality, consumed with herself and no one else. Yet there was an expression in her eyes that convinced me otherwise. She was listening intently to our conversation, but declined to participate. Was she shy? Or did she feel, like many beautiful women whose life path had been determined by their good looks, that she was intellectually inferior to others in her life, including her husband—*especially* her husband, who had made a point of belittling her intelligence?

As often happens when writers get together, most of the talk was about agents, money, publisher misdeeds, and other less literary topics. Chasseur held himself out as an expert on Hollywood and the transformation of books into motion pictures. He pontificated about it, citing his own experiences as proof of what he was saying. Eventually, he got on the subject of his publisher's lack of advertising and marketing support for his novels, and termed his agent "worthless." I expressed my satisfaction with both my publisher, Vaughan Buckley of Buckley House, one of the last remaining independently owned publishing companies in the business, and my agent of many years, Matt Miller.

"That's hopelessly naïve," Chausseur said. "You'll never know how much money they've stolen from you."

"I beg to differ—" I began.

My defense of my business colleagues was interrupted by an altercation at an adjacent table, where a man and a woman were engaged in a loud argument. All eyes in the vast dining room turned to them as the man abruptly stood, threw his napkin on the table, and stormed from the room. The woman started to cry, excused herself, and followed.

"Quite an unpleasant public display, I would say," Harold said.

I smiled. I recognized the man as Monroe, the actor playing the father at the rehearsal earlier in the day. "I think it's part of the show," I said softly, laughing.

"What show?" Chausseur said.

"It's part of the weekend's theatrical experience," I said, sorry that I'd brought it up. Who was I to spoil the fantasy that Melinda and Lawrence had created for Mohawk House that weekend?

The disruption was soon forgotten, and we went back to enjoying our dinner and discussing the financial pitfalls of writing for a living. But that lasted only a few minutes. The loud sound of gunfire, followed by a female scream, was heard from just outside the dining room. The small woman who'd argued with the redhead during check-in ran into the room, shouting, "Come quickly, please. He's got a gun!"

Chapter Five

*The characters Nero Wolfe and Archie Goodwin
resided in a brownstone on West Thirty-fifth
Street in Manhattan. Who created them?*

Many diners left the room to see what had happened,
and I was one of them. Although I was certain it had
to do with the play, I wanted to join in the scenario
Lawrence and Melinda Savoy had come up with for
the weekend. After all, that was half the fun of
being there.

The crowd had gathered in a large anteroom a few
feet down the hallway from the main entrance to
the dining room. I couldn't see the object of their
fascination until I managed to skirt the knot of people and stand on my tiptoes. I recognized Paul, Cynthia's suitor in the play and the young man with
whom I'd had a brief unpleasant encounter in the
smokers' vestibule. He was standing over an older
man slumped in an overstuffed chair. That man was
unknown to me. He hadn't been in the scene I'd
watched earlier during rehearsal.

"Don't think I'm not on to you," Paul shouted at
the man. He pointed his gun at the ceiling and

squeezed the trigger. The audience jumped at the loud explosion, although the bullet didn't make any hole in the plaster that I could see.

"What do you want?" the older man shouted at the young actor. "I don't know anything."

"Don't kid a kidder," Paul replied, waving the pistol in the man's face. "You know more than you're letting on. And I'm going to get every last detail from you if it takes all night."

At that moment, Mark Egmon pushed his way through the crowd. "What's going on here?" he demanded.

Paul immediately pocketed his weapon. "Just a slight disagreement," he said, glaring at his victim and daring him to contradict his story. He turned to the new man. "Who are you?"

"Mark Egmon, manager of special events here at Mohawk House. I heard someone had a gun. We don't allow firearms in the hotel."

Paul held up two empty hands. "Not me, Mr. Manager. As you can see, I'm unarmed."

Egmon looked from Paul to the man in the chair. "Does *he* have a gun?"

"No, sir," Paul replied. "He certainly does not."

"All right, then. There's no reason for this crowd to be here. C'mon, folks, break it up. Nothing to see here. Go finish your dinners. The dessert bar has been set up."

The man in the chair groaned and rubbed his chest with his right hand.

"What's wrong?" Egmon asked, squatting down beside the chair. "And you'd better not be complaining about the food."

"The food here is great," Paul said. "I tell everyone that." He nudged the man's leg with his foot. "What's the matter with you?"

The man groaned again. "Heart," he managed to get out in a pained voice.

Egmon jumped up and turned to the retreating crowd. "Is there a doctor in the house?"

Another man who'd come from the dining room stepped forward. "I'm a doctor," he said.

"Good," he said. "This man needs help."

With that, Egmon announced that he would call an ambulance, helped the actor to his feet, and propelled him away, the physician close on their heels. People who'd recognized that this was part of the show were laughing. The doctor, now aware that he'd been drawn into the play, also started to laugh, and gave a big, theatrical wave to the crowd on his way out.

As I turned to rejoin my writing colleagues in the dining room, I spotted Lawrence Savoy, who'd been watching the performance from a distance.

"What fun," I said to him.

He smiled. "Just the beginning, Jessica."

"How big a cast do you have?" I asked as we walked together into the dining room.

"Bigger than usual," he said. "We try to keep the number down to cut expenses. All the actors and actresses are in the Actors Equity union. But Melinda wrote this new play and got carried away with characters. I've been using a few hotel staff to fill in, like Egmon, who helped Harry off the stage just now. You know Mark. A really nice guy. I think he wanted to be an actor somewhere in his past."

"Well," I said pleasantly, "don't get any thoughts about using me in your production."

He feigned shock. "I had you written in, Jessica, as the one who solves the murder."

"I've solved too many murders in real life to be doing it in a play. Thanks, but no thanks, Larry—I mean Lawrence."

Savoy laughed. "Come on, Jessica. We've known each other too long to stand on ceremony. You're welcome to call me Larry. Just not in public." He winked.

"I'll try to remember that," I said. "Joining us again at the table?"

"No, too much to do to get ready for the first act tonight. Having a good time?"

"Of course. I always do at your shows."

"Enjoying the other writers?"

My hesitation wasn't lost on Larry.

"Egotistical bunch, I admit," he said with a straight face, "but they are, after all, writers."

"I beg your pardon?"

He laughed. "Just getting a rise from you. Chasseur was a last-minute addition to the author panel. He'd been bugging me for a month to be part of this weekend. When Tony Tedeschi—you know him, don't you?"

"Yes. A wonderful writer and a nice person."

"When Tony had to cancel a week ago—some family emergency—I called Chasseur. He's arrogant, but he can be entertaining."

"Yes, he is," I said pleasantly. "Both."

"Looks like we literally have a captive audience," he said. "With this storm raging outside, they couldn't leave if they wanted to. I just heard an updated forecast. *More* than two feet of snow."

"If I didn't know better," I said, "I'd think I was back in Maine."

Melinda came up to us and pulled Larry away to handle what she described as a crisis. I returned to the table, where only GSB Wick and Harold remained.

"You missed the excitement," I said as Harold stood to pull out my chair.

"I don't believe we were *formally* introduced," he said, slurring his words and rocking on his feet. "Harold Boynton here." He pointed at his chest and settled his heavy body back into his chair. "Not very polite of me not to have introduced myself."

"Ms. Wick took care of introductions," I said.

"Boynton, you're drunk again," Georgie said with disgust. To me, she added, "I'm going to beg to be excused. I'm not feeling well."

Her pale makeup hid the true nature of her complexion, but she did look wan to me.

"I'm so sorry," I said. "Is there anything I can get you?"

"Nothing at all," she said. "What I need is to lie down."

Boynton struggled to his feet and took her hand as she rose.

"You stay with Jessica, Harold," she said. "I'm going to bed." She put a hand to her forehead. "I hope I'm not getting the flu."

I glanced down at the two empty cocktail glasses in front of her, and wondered whether it was the alcohol that had made her ill. Harold made another attempt to escort her from the room, but she was adamant that he stay with me.

"I'm sure you'll feel better after a good night's sleep," I said.

"I hope you're right," she said and walked away, her painfully thin body moving unsteadily.

"I love her writing," I told Harold after he was seated again.

"Yes, she's jolly good, isn't she?" he said.

"She certainly is. So, Harold Boynton, what do you do back in England?"

"Retired. Physician," he said, muffling a burp behind his napkin.

"Oh? One of my dearest friends back home—that's in a town called Cabot Cove—it's in Maine—is a physician."

"Might I know him?"

"I doubt it."

"What's his name?"

"Seth Hazlitt."

"Doesn't ring a bell. What's his specialty?"

"Medicine," I said with a chuckle. "He's a true country physician, an old-fashioned general practitioner. He calls himself a chicken soup doctor."

Harold joined my laughter. "An endangered species," he said, "and too bad."

"Did you specialize when you were in practice?" I asked.

"Yes, quite so. I was a coroner and medical examiner. Your friend, Dr. Hazlitt, tries to save people's lives. I chop them up when he fails."

I'd never heard a coroner or medical examiner describe his specialty quite so crudely before. I'd had the privilege of meeting many top medical examiners, including Michael Baden and Henry Lee, in the course of research I'd done for my novels. They tended to be gentle when describing what they do, speaking of the deceased with a certain reverence, anatomical and surgical nomenclature aside.

"Like to go dancing, Jessica, dear?" he asked, leaning toward my ear. "I understand they have a lively pub here in the hotel. We could sneak away together."

"No, thank you, Harold, I don't think so. I brought a good book with me—Ms. Wick's latest, as a matter of fact. And one by Mr. Chasseur, too."

"Pity," he said, tapping my arm. "I'd like to get to know you better, Jessica." He placed a hand on the top of my thigh.

I lifted it away by the sleeve, placed it back on the arm of his chair, and stood. "I believe the play is about to start," I said, "and I don't want to miss any of it."

Feeling like one of Larry's actors, I made my exit, stage right.

As I went to the auditorium, I passed the young actor who played Paul in the play. It was almost curtain time, and although he was in makeup and wearing his stage clothing, I wondered why he wasn't backstage, ready to perform. As he hurried past me, a young woman grabbed his arm to stop him. "Hey, Peter," she said, "I didn't know you'd be here."

Paul glared at her, yanked his arm free, and said, "You've got me confused with somebody else. Sorry, I'm in a hurry."

Paul disappeared into a knot of theatergoers, leaving the woman looking puzzled. She saw that I'd witnessed the exchange, laughed, and said, "He's a dead ringer for someone I knew back in San Francisco."

"It's happened to me on a few occasions," I said, walking into the theater with her, "and seems to happen more frequently as I've grown older. I don't think it's because my ability to recognize people has diminished. There just seem to be more faces that look familiar to me."

"Well," she said as she found a seat, "they say everyone has a twin somewhere in the world, and that guy could be my friend's twin. Enjoy the show."

Chapter Six

Who wrote the hard-boiled detective novel
I, the Jury?

There was an air of excitement and expectation among the hundred or so people entering the auditorium for the first act of the play. I've learned over the years how devoted serious lovers of murder mysteries can be. They read every book in the genre they can get their hands on, and have rock-solid opinions about the relative quality of authors, plots, character development, and other aspects of the field. They love arguing with other devotees, and spend countless hours in Internet chat rooms and at conventions dedicated to crime writing.

I took a seat toward the rear of the room and eavesdropped on conversations around me. The teams had already begun to gather in clusters and to conjure scenarios. The talk—at least what I could pick up—was about Paul and the man in the chair outside the dining room a half hour earlier. Obviously, this incident would have significance as the theatrical production went forward, although at this early stage its importance was entirely speculative, especially since no one knew who these men were or what roles they would assume in the play.

Lawrence Savoy stepped onto the small stage. "Good evening, ladies and gentlemen, lovers all of a good mystery."

The buzz in the room continued until Larry called for attention. Conversation wound down and he continued with his introduction: "Welcome to the magnificent Mohawk House and a weekend of merry mayhem, dastardly crimes, and murder most foul. And we won't let this snowstorm dampen our spirits, will we?"

A chorus of affirmation welled up.

"As you know," Larry continued, "we'll begin each of our sessions with a few questions devised by our distinguished authors to test your knowledge of the murder mystery genre. At the end of the weekend, the person with the most correct answers will win a special prize. Everybody should have a card." He held up a sample of the small index cards that had been distributed. "You'll write your answers on the cards provided in your welcoming packets and they'll be collected before the play begins. Be sure to write your name on them so you'll be able to pick them up the next time we gather. No changing your answers allowed. If we see an erasure, you're disqualified. No consulting the Internet. And turn off your cell phones now."

He read off the first set of questions, and everyone around me began writing. Many, concerned that their answers might be copied, used their bodies, as well as other materials they'd brought into the room, to shield their cards from other eyes. A few minutes later, Melinda Savoy and some of the hotel staff circulated among the attendees and collected the cards.

"All right," Larry said into his handheld microphone, "it's time for the fun to begin. As many of you know, an altercation took place less than an hour ago. One of the participants is being treated by the kindly physician who stepped forward in the best tradition of medicine. The gentleman who'd fallen ill claims he's being blackmailed. I've placed a call to the local police, but either they're all out to dinner, or have other crimes to investigate. I'll let you know the minute they arrive—and, I must warn you, everyone in this room will be considered a suspect. One of you may be a blackmailer. Blackmail is a terrible crime, but there are some that are even worse. And before the night is over, you may witness another heinous crime."

He delivered that last line in an ominous tone, which elicited moans of foreboding from the audience.

"So sit back, relax, and remember: You never know whether or not the person seated next to you is a blackmailer—or a cold-blooded killer. Beware! And good luck to all."

The curtain behind Larry slowly opened, revealing the drawing room set in which Monroe and Victoria Whittaker, their daughter, Cynthia, and her young suitor, Paul, were gathered.

"Feel like taking a walk?" Paul asked Cynthia. He then whispered, "Let's get out of here."

"What a grand idea," she said. "It's such a nice night to take a walk. I hear there's a full moon."

"You won't see any moon," Monroe Whittaker declared. "Not with the fog out there. Besides, there's still snow on the ground, and more in the forecast."

"That's okay, Daddy," Cynthia said. "It's so warm in here with the fire going. I could really use some fresh air. I'm sure Paul could, too. Besides, you always say a walk after dinner is good for your digestion. Isn't that how you put it?"

Victoria Whittaker said to Paul, "We have a very busy day tomorrow with the attorneys coming. Cynthia will need a clear head. I want to be sure she gets enough rest. Make sure you don't keep her out late again."

"He won't," Cynthia said, kissing her mother's cheek. They put on outerwear. She grabbed Paul's hand and led him through French doors to the outside. "Let's look for that moon, anyway."

"Be careful, Cynthia," a woman in the audience called out.

Another audience member shushed her.

"I don't trust him," said a man from the audience.

"I haven't changed my mind," Monroe Whittaker said from the stage. "I don't like him."

"That's patently obvious," said his wife, checking her hair in a mirror over the fireplace. "But the least you can do is be civil to him this weekend."

"Civil?" Monroe snorted. "How about if I pack his

bag and send him away from here? Would that be civil enough?"

"Monroe, you're not thinking clearly. Cynthia is like all young women her age. She's rebelling against us because it's the thing to do. I share your opinion of Paul. He's obviously not of Cynthia's class. I'll give him credit for trying to dress the part, although anyone can see the poor quality of his clothes."

"He looked pretty good to me," a woman sitting in front of me murmured to her companions. "I don't care if his sweater isn't cashmere. Did you see those muscles? I like a man with a good build."

"Not a bad face either," her friend replied.

"Shhh, both of you," said another woman. "Everything they say may be a clue. I don't want to miss anything." She scribbled furiously on her pad.

"His father is a policeman in New York City. Good Lord, you know how crude policemen can be," Victoria was saying.

"A cop? How do you know that?"

"I don't recall exactly. Does it matter? He must have told me. But the point is that the more we challenge the young man, the more we'll push Cynthia into the relationship. Trust me, darling, the best way to see the last of him is to shower him with kindness and expose him to our daughter's lifestyle and breeding. He'll become uncomfortable soon enough and seek his own kind. I think I'll go up. Are you coming?"

"Not yet," he growled.
With that, Victoria left Monroe alone on the stage.

People throughout the room took copious notes, causing me to smile. From my past experience with productions mounted by Larry and Melinda Savoy, I knew how seriously those in attendance took their responsibility to solve the crime at the end of the weekend. Some would fill entire notebooks and spend half the night with fellow team members charting the scenes from the play on blackboards or on huge pads of presentation paper. Someone passing too close to one of these analytical sessions would cause all conversation to cease, and two or three team members would quickly step in front of the graphic representation to block it from view. Multiple pairs of eyes would follow the progress of the intruder, waiting until he or she was well out of earshot before resuming the arguments, piecing together the myriad clues dropped during the play and at offstage goings-on that permeated every aspect of the weekend stay at Mohawk House.

"Damn fog," Whittaker muttered, walking over to the desk. He slammed his fist on the desktop, reached into a desk drawer, withdrew a bulky envelope that he shoved into the pocket of his smoking jacket, and stormed out the French doors.

As he left, a maid entered the room through another door and proceeded to dust furniture and rummage through the desk until the sound of Victoria's voice in the next room sent her hastily back to dusting. She was only a minute into her chores when the snap of a weapon being discharged from somewhere outside shattered the stillness onstage. A woman's piercing scream sounded from the wings.

Cynthia burst through the doors. "Help!" she shouted. "Someone help me!"

Paul then stumbled into the room, one hand pressed against his chest, blood oozing through his fingers. He had a wild look on his face, as though desperately seeking help from someone, anyone. His other hand reached out in a pleading gesture, palm up, arm trembling uncontrollably, going from person to person.

It struck me as a bit of overacting, but others in the audience responded differently.

The women in front of me gasped. "It looks so realistic," one of them said.

"Nuts! I was hoping he wouldn't be the one. I was going to interview him first. Now we'll never see him again till the last day when he takes a bow."

"Maybe they'll let him join the reception in the bar anyway. We could ask him why he died."

"They don't do that. Only the living cast members are allowed to join the guests."

The maid had rushed from the room, replaced by the Whittakers. Paul fell to his knees at Cynthia's feet. With a final, agonizing rale, he pitched forward, his face coming to rest on the floor, neatly avoiding her shoe.

"Daddy," Cynthia shrieked, and collapsed into her father's arms, sobbing.

"Is he dead?" Victoria asked calmly.

Monroe scowled down at the body on the floor and looked over to his wife. "Yes, I'd say he's dead. Very dead."

The groans and general murmur from the audience were quieted when the doors to the auditorium were flung open and two men boldly stepped into the room. One wore a tan trench coat, and a fedora was perched on his head at a rakish angle. The second man wore a policeman's blue uniform.

"Don't nobody move!" the plainclothes cop shouted.

"Don't nobody move!" the uniformed cop said.

"I already said that," the cop wearing the trench coat admonished his colleague.

As they swaggered up to the stage, the uniformed cop waved a handgun back and forth, causing some audience members to duck.

The plainclothes officer faced the crowd. "All right," he said. "Who's in charge here?"

"This is my home," Monroe Whittaker said.

"Who are you?"

"Monroe Whittaker. And who are you, sir?"

"Detective first-class Nick Carboroni, and this moron with me is Officer no-class Clarence Dolt."

A wave of laughter greeted the comical pair, easing the tension that had been established by the murder.

Carboroni scowled at the crowd. "You think this is funny? You spend the day with this dimwit and you'll see how funny it ain't. His elevator don't go all the way to the top. Know what I mean?'' He pointed at his temple and rolled his eyes.

Clarence Dolt pulled on the detective's sleeve. ''Detective? Why are we here?''

''Why are we here? I got a call that somebody was waving around a gun here tonight. That's why we're here.''

''I got a gun,'' Dolt said, waving his pistol and pointing it at the detective.

Carboroni swatted his hand. ''Cut it out.''

Lawrence Savoy stepped from the wings. ''A man was being threatened with a pistol earlier this evening. He's being treated for chest pains as we speak.''

''He ain't dead?'' Dolt asked disappointedly, still waving the pistol.

''Put that thing away,'' Carboroni said, ''before you kill somebody.'' To Savoy: ''Who's the perperpertruder?''

''The what?'' Savoy said. ''Oh, you mean who threatened him with the gun? We don't know.''

Carboroni approached onlookers in the first row and started to question them about what they'd seen that night. When one elderly gentleman seemed at a loss for words, Officer Dolt stuck his gun in the man's face, prompting Carboroni to yell at him to holster his weapon. The mock questioning of audience members continued, the detectives' ad-libs causing lots of laughter in the room.

All attention, of course, was on the comic scene playing out at the front of the room. While the questioning continued, Officer Dolt wandered up onto the stage, saw Paul still prone on the floor, turned, and said, "Hey, Detective, maybe you better take a look-see here."

Carboroni spun around and said, "How many times do I have to tell you not to interrupt me when I'm interrogarating people?" Then he saw Paul's body on the stage, excused himself from the audience, and joined Dolt.

"Who's this?" Carboroni asked Whittaker.

"My daughter's *former* suitor," Whittaker replied, sounding pleased.

"That you?" the detective said to Cynthia.

She responded by letting out a bloodcurdling wail and running from the stage. Her mother, Victoria, had collapsed on the couch, where she fanned herself with a magazine.

Carboroni nudged his toe into Paul's side. "Hey, where'd you get shot?"

There was no response from the fallen actor.

Carboroni asked Larry Savoy, "Is this the man who was threatened earlier in the evening?"

"No, Detective," Larry said.

It all sounded like scripted banter, but I sensed something was wrong. From my vantage point, I could tell that Paul hadn't moved a muscle since stumbling into the scene and falling at Cynthia's feet. The pool of fake blood had been widening. I saw a stricken look come over Larry Savoy's face as he looked down at Paul. He motioned to Melinda in the wings, and the curtain began to close. Victoria, sensing something was wrong, rose from the couch and bent down to peer at Paul. She straightened, wailed, "Oh, my God!" and fell into Larry's arms.

"What's goin' on here?" Carboroni asked.

The actor playing Monroe Whittaker came to Paul, crouched, and placed his fingers against Paul's neck. He slowly stood and raised two bloodstained fingers.

Victoria sniffled. "Is he dead?" she asked.

"Yes, I'd say he's dead," her stage husband intoned.

Chapter Seven

What British mystery writer also writes psychological crime novels under the pseudonym Barbara Vine?

Confusion reigned.

Because a play had been in progress, the audience assumed what they'd just witnessed was part of the script, and considered Paul's "demise" to be a theatrical event. Many team members busily took notes and engaged in intense discussions about who in the cast might have shot Paul. Monroe Whittaker was the obvious suspect, but these savvy murder mystery buffs knew that other possibilities would emerge as the weekend progressed.

I didn't share their illusions. Something tragic—something *real*—had just taken place before the curtain fell, and it had nothing to do with the script. I made my way to the stage, went up three short steps, and slipped backstage, where the scene was chaotic. The actor playing Paul lay where he'd fallen, his blood penetrating the wooden floor, creating a dark red aura about his lifeless body.

Larry Savoy was trying to calm everyone down. "Please," he said. "Hysteria isn't going to help anyone, especially Paul. Come on, come on, everyone, there's nothing to be gained by standing around. Go back to the dressing room, and for God's sake, don't say anything about this to the hotel guests if you want to get paid this weekend."

Mark Egmon, Mohawk House's special-events manager, burst through the curtains. "What happened?" he asked no one in particular. "There's a rumor he's really dead. Is it true?"

"We need an ambulance," Larry answered, putting his arm around Egmon's shoulder and moving him away from Paul's inert form.

"What you need is a coroner," Monroe muttered.

Larry shot him an angry look, but it was too late. Egmon had overheard Monroe. He wrung his hands and looked from person to person. "This is horrendous," he said. "Nothing like this has happened at Mohawk House. The only deaths we ever experienced were from natural causes—a heart attack, a stroke. Who could have done such a thing? Why did it have to happen here?"

"That will be up to the police to determine," Savoy said.

Egmon turned to the actor playing the uniformed officer in the mystery, who still held a revolver. "Are you—?"

The actor raised his arm, inadvertently pointing the weapon at Egmon. The manager stepped backward, his hands extended in a defensive position.

"Put that down," Savoy said to the pretend cop.

To Egmon he said, "You'd better get some real cops here as fast as possible."

"Nobody touch nothing," the actor portraying Detective Carboroni ordered.

"Oh, shut up," Savoy said. "Monroe, give me your jacket."

Monroe stroked one hand down his lapel. "This is a genuine silk smoking jacket, Lawrence. Tell me you're not going to do what I think you're suggesting."

Larry held out his hand. "Whittaker—the jacket."

"If you get blood on it, I won't wear it again. That I can promise you."

"Wardrobe will get you another one. Now hurry up."

Monroe slipped off the smoking jacket and hooked one finger in the collar to pass it to Savoy. The ascot at his neck looked strange against his sleeveless ribbed undershirt.

Larry placed the jacket over Paul so that it covered his head. There was an audible sigh from several cast members. Despite the horror of murder, shielding the dead body from view made it less painful for those in attendance. "I'll stay until the police arrive to make sure nothing is touched," Larry said. "The rest of you get out of here. The audience should be at the reception in the bar by now. You know what you have to do."

Egmon said, "Oh, I'm not sure about this. I'll have to check with others in management."

"You have to call the police, remember?"

"Of course," Egmon said, looking back over his shoulder at Paul's body. He pulled a cell phone from his pocket and rushed off the stage.

"Lawrence," Victoria said, wiping her eyes with a tissue. "You can't expect us to carry on as if nothing has happened. Look at my hands. They're shaking. How can I hide it? The audience may suspect the truth. They'll ask us questions."

"That's what they're supposed to do," Larry said, looking at each member of the cast, "and you'll answer them in character. And if you shed a tear in talking about Paul, they will assume you're the best actor they've ever met. Now, find Cynthia and tell her what I said. No one talks about this unless they're in character, and keep Paul's situation fictitious. Understood?"

The actors nodded, and one by one shuffled off the stage.

"Nicely done," said a voice from the wings after Egmon and the cast had departed the stage. John Chasseur sauntered into the light. "Have you felt for a pulse? The victim may not be gone yet."

"Of course he's 'gone,'" said GSB Wick, who'd slipped through the slit in the curtains. "I could see that from the front row. If he didn't die from the wound, he probably croaked from the loss of blood. He's been lying there a while."

Obviously, Georgie had made a hasty recovery from the flu she'd felt coming on. Perhaps her momentary malaise had been an excuse to get away from her companion, Harold, the randy coroner. If so, I certainly understood her need to remove herself.

"I'm disappointed," Chasseur said haughtily. "You've started without me."

"I can't believe this," Larry mumbled to me.

"Looks like you'd better," I said.

Chasseur came to where the body lay and picked up the sleeve of Monroe's smoking jacket to get a better view. He lifted Paul's shoulder to expose the wound, which was in the middle of the chest. "He was supposed to be killed as part of the play, wasn't he?" he asked, letting the body fall back onto the floor.

"Right," Larry said. "And you'd better stop touching things." He looked at me. "Right, Jess?"

"Absolutely," I said. "The police will be very unhappy if they know the crime scene isn't pristine."

"Don't lecture me," Chasseur said, kneeling and feeling Paul's wrist for a pulse.

"Who was supposed to fire the weapon?" I asked Larry.

He hesitated. "One of the tech crew, I'm not sure who. Easy to find out. Melinda knows. She's in charge of offstage business."

"Is the weapon you use in the production capable of firing live ammunition as well as blanks?" I asked.

"Yes, but we only load blanks and use minimal powder."

My change of expression must have concerned him because he asked, "What's the matter, Jess?"

"I was just thinking that whoever did this might

be long gone from Mohawk House by now. It's a shame there wasn't a way to contain everyone within the hotel."

"Chances are the frightful weather has done a good job of that. But I'll get Egmon to station his people at the exits," Larry said, sounding grateful he had a reason to leave. "Maybe the killer hasn't had a chance to escape yet."

"He's definitely dead," Chasseur said, standing and pulling a white handkerchief from his back pocket. He wiped his hands, although there'd been no blood on Paul's shoulder or wrist.

"Do you think the killer's escaped already?" Georgie asked. She'd been keeping her distance from Paul's body.

"With the barn door open, I'll bet that horse is already gone," Chasseur said.

"Maybe, maybe not," I said. "If the killer is staying in the hotel, it might raise less suspicion to simply stay put."

Georgie offered, "The killer might be milling around with the people who're still out there." She pointed to the curtain.

"Are people still in the auditorium?" I asked.

She nodded, her pale face even more ashen under the harsh stage lights.

"Let me see what I can do," I said.

I parted the heavy curtain and descended the stairs to where a dozen hangers-on were gathered in a tight circle, whispering among themselves. I hoped our backstage conversations hadn't carried out to the auditorium. Whoever shot Paul couldn't be certain if he was dead, or had merely been wounded. That possibility, coupled with the blizzard raging outside, might keep the killer from leaving. The only road leading up to Mohawk House was at least four miles long and full of hairpin turns, steep inclines, and dangerous drop-offs.

The minute they saw me emerge from backstage, they converged and asked whether it was true that someone had been shot to death.

I held up my hands. "There's been an unfortunate accident with one of the cast members," I said, working hard to sustain calm in my voice. "An ambulance has been called for. The police have been summoned, and I suggest we all stay away from this area until they arrive."

The questions flew: "Is he dead?" "Do they have the gun?" "Do they have the shooter?" "Has it really happened, or is this part of the play?"

One woman shook her finger at me and said, "You naughty devil, Jessica Fletcher. You're just saying what you're supposed to say as part of the play. You don't fool me."

I was happy to see Mark Egmon enter the room. I excused myself and went over to him.

"The police are on their way," Mark told me, "provided they can get up the road." He kept his voice low to avoid being overheard. "And I spoke with a couple of the management team members about how to handle this. We're scheduled to meet again in a half hour to formulate plans. What's going on backstage?"

"Nothing for you to be concerned about, Mark. I'll certainly feel better when the police arrive and secure the crime scene. It's already been contaminated."

"By whom?"

"It doesn't matter. In the meantime, you might consider clearing this room. When the police arrive, they—"

The doors opened and two uniformed officers entered. Following behind them was a young man wearing a heavy red and black plaid wool jacket, jeans, a fur hat of the sort seen on Russian Cossacks, and pale yellow ankle-high boots. He brushed snow from his shoulders and arms and introduced himself as Detective Dwayne Ladd.

"Where's the deceased?" the officer in the plaid wool jacket asked in a nasal voice.

"On the stage, behind the curtains," Egmon said, pointing at the stairs.

There was a gasp from one of the audience members. A woman standing close enough to hear started to cry. Her friend consoled her. "For heaven's sakes, Gertrude. This is still part of the play. Don't you see? No real detective looks like that."

"You think?" The sniffling woman looked the detective up and down, and smiled at her companion.

"Get them out of here," the detective said.

Mark Egmon ushered the few stragglers in the auditorium out the back door, consoling them in comforting tones, answering questions diplomatically, and reassuring them that they were safe at the hotel. I stayed back, trying to catch the detective's attention.

As the police walked toward the stage, I called after them, "Excuse me, Detective."

He stopped, turned. "Yes?"

"It might be a good idea to seal off the hotel."

He cocked his head and squinted, as though trying to bring something fuzzy into focus. "Who are you?" he asked.

"My name is Jessica Fletcher. I don't mean to intrude, but whoever did the shooting may be planning to leave the premises. That could have happened already, I admit, but it would be prudent to take precautions in any event."

His squint was accompanied by a frown, which rendered his face prunelike. For a moment, I thought he might lash out at me for injecting myself into what was his bailiwick. Instead, his face softened almost into a smile. "Good suggestion, Mrs.—what did you say your name was?"

"Fletcher. Jessica Fletcher."

"The mystery writer?"

"Yes. I—"

"You're here for this mystery weekend, right? I saw your picture in the paper."

"That's right, but aren't we wasting valuable time discussing this?"

The squint and frown returned. He turned to the uniformed officers and said, "Get outside and make sure nobody leaves the hotel. Get some backup here and cover every exit. And do it fast before we get enough snow to close the mountain road."

"There's a downstairs door in the rear that leads outside," I called to the officers' backs as they exited the room.

Detective Ladd walked to the stairs leading to the stage. After a moment's debate, I decided to follow, but observed from a distance as the detective encountered my writing colleagues and Larry Savoy, who had returned backstage.

Ladd removed Monroe's smoking jacket, and bent down on one knee to observe the victim and his wound at close range. He stood. "When did the shooting take place?"

Larry stepped forward. "A half hour ago maybe," he said, introducing himself and proceeding to fill Ladd in on the details of what had occurred.

"He was supposed to get shot in the play," Chasseur put in.

"It's written into the script," Georgie Wick added. "The gun's only supposed to shoot blanks."

"Are you all in the cast?" Ladd asked. "You look familiar."

Chasseur pointed to his T-shirt and the illustration depicting the cover of his latest novel. "John Chasseur, best-selling novelist."

"You write the Agent Benny series," Ladd said. "I've heard of you."

Chasseur faked a modest smile.

Ladd looked at Georgie. "Are you a writer, too?"

She gave a small, uncertain smile. "GSB Wick. You've probably never heard of me."

He pointed at her and squinted. "Yeah," he said. "I know the name. And weren't you on *Regis* once?"

She looked relieved. "Yes, and the *Today* show, too."

He swept a hand around the stage, his gaze going from face to face. "You're all here for the mystery weekend, huh? Isn't that ironic? Murder mystery writers. And now you have a real murder instead of the ones you make up." He paused. "Interesting."

Lawrence Savoy cleared his throat.

"Right," Ladd said to him. "You're the producer. You have the gun?"

"No, but I called my wife on my cell phone a few minutes ago. She'll bring it."

Ladd became aware that I was standing behind him. "Mrs. Fletcher," he said, "you seem to know a lot about what happened here."

"Oh, no," I said, closing the gap between us. "I hope you weren't offended that I injected myself the way I did, but it seemed to me that—"

"It's okay," the detective said. "You were right."

"What did she tell you?" Chasseur demanded. "She doesn't know any more than the rest of us. We were watching the play, too. Our powers of observation are every bit as good as hers."

"Of course, I'm not as experienced with violent crime as my distinguished colleagues," Georgie said, "but I'll be happy to tell you what I saw."

I hadn't realized till then that Chasseur, and Georgie to a lesser extent, was competing with me for Detective Ladd's attention. Fortunately, at that moment Melinda Savoy came from the opposite side of the stage, accompanied by the young woman who'd tried to keep guests from invading the stage that afternoon. All eyes turned in their direction. Melinda carried a handgun, holding it by her fingertips as far away from her body as possible, as though it might bite. She handed the weapon to Detective Ladd, who pulled a handkerchief from his pocket before touching it.

"Is that the murder weapon?" Georgie asked before Ladd could get a word out.

"No," Melinda replied. "I mean, it's a stage prop. It makes noise, but we only shoot blanks."

"Then you don't have to bother worrying about fingerprints with that thing," Chasseur said.

"So, where's the weapon that shot a real bullet into the victim?" Ladd asked Melinda.

She shrugged and looked at Larry, who did the same thing.

"Who are you?" Georgie asked the young woman with Melinda.

"Laura Tehaar. I'm in charge of props and costumes."

"And?" Chasseur prompted, walking to her side.

"I was supposed to fire the gun when the script calls for it," she said, looking up at him.

"You didn't?" Georgie asked, coming to her other side.

Laura swung her face toward Georgie.

"Wait a minute, wait a minute," Ladd said, waving his hands as though to physically push them away. "All of you, back off. I'm the detective here. I'll ask the questions." He gave Chasseur and Georgie stern looks. They appeared to be annoyed, but stepped back.

Ladd coughed before asking Laura, "Did you fire the gun when the script called for it?"

"Yes, sir." She started to cry, and Melinda wrapped her arms about her.

"What's the deceased's name?"

"Paul Brody," Larry offered.

"Paul's the name of the character," Chasseur said. "Is that his real name?"

"Or stage name?" Georgie added.

Ladd shot them an angry look. He turned to Larry and raised his eyebrows.

"It's his real name," Larry said. "We use the actors' real names for their roles whenever possible. It makes it more natural for them to respond to questions from the hotel guests. When the actors are off-stage, they're still required to stay in character. That's part of the mystery experience. The guests ask the actors questions about the plotlines, and they answer as if they're actually the person in the play. If someone calls out 'Paul,' he's going to turn around. It's his name after all." Larry hesitated. "Or was."

Melinda added, "There are exceptions. Our two police officers use stage names, Carboroni and Dolt."

"I'd hope those aren't their real names," Ladd said through what passed for a laugh.

Mark Egmon rejoined us on the stage. "We have a lot of people lingering outside the auditorium," he told the detective. "They expect to be questioned and they're getting restless. I also have a few who want to check out immediately. The play was too gruesome, they said. I'd appreciate some guidance on how to proceed."

Ladd rubbed his chin. "Okay," he said. "You'll have to tell everybody that no one can leave until they've been questioned."

"There's more than a hundred guests, Detective," Egmon said, his voice mirroring his dismay.

"Can't be helped," said Ladd. His cell phone rang. "All right," he said after listening to the caller. "All the exits are covered. The ME's on her way—if she can make it through the snow."

One of the uniformed officers entered, and Ladd directed him to guard the body. "Don't let anyone near him. Got it?"

The officer patted his holster and positioned himself near the corpse, standing spread-legged as if ready to take on any and all attackers.

"I'll be back," Ladd said, and left with Egmon, Chasseur, and Georgie trailing after him.

I went to where Larry, Melinda, and Laura stood in a tight circle. Melinda had tried to retrieve Monroe's jacket, but the officer waved her away. "Don't mess with the scene," he'd said.

"What do you think, Jessica?"

"About what, Larry?"

"About getting through the rest of the weekend. We might as well pack up and get out of here."

"I don't think that's an option," I said. "It's a police matter now. You heard the detective. No one can leave until they've been questioned, and that will include you and the other members of the troupe." *Especially the troupe*, I thought.

"I know, I know," he said. "I'm still in shock. I'm not thinking clearly. I only know I can't believe any of my people had anything to do with this."

"I'm surprised at you, Larry," Melinda said. "We're actors. The show must go on. You can't call it off. We'd have a lot of angry people—and not just cast members."

"If it gets out that Paul is really dead, people might be angrier that we're going forward," he said, chewing his lip. He looked at Laura. "What do you think?"

She glanced at Paul's body, sniffled, and straightened her shoulders. "If the show must go on, I won't let you down," she said. "I'll do whatever you decide."

Larry sighed.

"I don't envy you making the decision," I said. I wandered over to the wings and peered into the gloom backstage. I glanced up at the line of spotlights with different colored gels covering the bulbs and at the scaffolding to which they were attached.

"Melinda, you're right," Larry said, pacing back and forth in front of the body. "The show should go on. But, of course, that decision won't be ours to make. I'll ask Mohawk House management what they want us to do. I'll leave it up to them."

"They're going to want us to go forward," Melinda said. "They stand to lose a lot of money if all the guests check out after they're questioned by the police. And don't forget, we do, too. We still have to pay the cast, according to Equity rules. Not to mention the cost of their transportation and all the props and costumes we rented for this weekend. No, we can't quit. The show has to go on. You have to convince them of that." She turned to me. "Don't you think I'm right, Jessica?"

"Hmmm? I'm sorry. I wasn't listening. I had a thought."

"What is it?" Melinda asked.

"I was thinking—and I know this may sound outlandish, even ghoulish—but I was thinking that your play might help point to the young man's murderer."

"Really?" Melinda said. "How?"

"I'm not sure," I said. "Just an instinct."

"Your instincts have always been pretty good," Larry said.

"And sometimes they haven't," I said. "But in this case, they might pass the test. Everyone is captive here at Mohawk House until Detective Ladd is satisfied. The snowstorm plays a role, too, in keeping them here. The paying guests are going to have an awful lot of time on their hands, and you know what that can result in. I think continuing with the play will serve two purposes. First, it will calm those who suspect that a murder truly took place. Second—and this is certainly more important—it might—and I emphasize *might*—shed some light on the murder and the murderer."

"See?" Melinda said. "Jessica agrees. The show must go on."

"But what about the detective?" Larry asked. "Will *he* go along with it?"

"You can ask."

"I'll take a shot at it."

"Poor choice of words," Melinda said as the medical examiner, two white-coated assistants, and a crime scene tech arrived, along with Detective Ladd, followed by his mystery author attendants.

As we were leaving the scene in the hands of the professionals, I asked Detective Ladd if he could find a few minutes to speak with me.

"About what?" he asked.

"About an idea I have that might help you solve this terrible crime."

The squint and frown crossed his face again.

"I would really appreciate it, Detective."

"Okay," he said, taking my elbow and leading me into the wings. "I need ten minutes with the ME. After that I'll look for you, but I hope you won't waste my time with some cockamamie scheme like your friends over there." He nodded at Chasseur and Wick.

"I'll certainly try not to," I said, not at all sure that that wasn't exactly what I was doing.

Chapter Eight

The Postman Always Rings Twice *was published in 1934. Who wrote it?*

Mark Egmon intercepted me as I left. "Can we talk?" he asked.

"Sure."

We went in a small library in which floor-to-ceiling bookcases lined one wall and a movable ladder afforded access to the top shelves. Two red leather chairs flanked a table; a Tiffany lamp on it provided the room's only illumination. Mark closed the door and we sat.

"I'm absolutely in shock," he said.

"Murder is always shocking," I said.

"Shocked or not, we have a lot of decisions to make."

"I imagine you do."

"The police have sealed off all the doors, and that has some of the guests upset. No, that's an understatement. A few are already clamoring for their money back."

"I'm sure they'll understand that it isn't management's decision. It's a police matter."

"You're being rational, Jessica. Interesting, though,

how some who suspect a real murder has taken place want very much to stay and help solve the crime. They considerate it some sort of a bonus for the weekend, an added value." He shook his head. "I've been toying with the idea of moving the author panel to tomorrow morning, maybe even later tonight. Seeing how calmly you and the other writers are taking the situation might rub off."

"That's not a bad idea, Mark, but I should mention that I've suggested to the Savoys that we proceed with the entire weekend as planned."

"All of it? The show, too?"

"Yes."

I explained my thinking and he listened attentively. When I was finished, he said, "I buy it, Jessica. I don't know if others in management will, but I'll try to convince them."

"Good. Larry Savoy was going to speak to his cast members to see if they're willing, considering the tragedy that's taken place."

"And I'll talk to my bosses. I may ask you to weigh in with them."

"I'll be happy to do anything I can. The biggest hurdle might be Detective Ladd. If he feels it will get in the way of his investigation, he'll veto the idea."

"Hopefully, he'll listen to you."

I left the library and found the detective in the main lobby conferring with other officers. Dozens of guests milled about, many obviously wanting to speak with him, but most, including me, had the good sense to give him a wide berth.

Ladd eventually became aware of my presence and came over to me, ignoring others trying to capture his attention. "You said you had something to talk to me about," he said. "An idea you have?"

"Yes, Detective. I appreciate your taking the time."

We went along the hallway to a relatively secluded alcove.

"So," he said, "what's this idea? You'll have to make it quick."

I outlined my reasons for allowing the theatrical production to continue as planned. If I judged his reaction by the sour look on his thin face, my idea didn't have a chance of being accepted. But to my surprise, he said, "Makes sense to me, Mrs. Fletcher. But the minute it gets in the way of my investigation, it's over."

"Understandable," I said. "I'll make sure the Savoys, the show's producers, keep everyone out of your hair."

A small smile crossed his lips as he touched the thinning reddish hair on top of his head. "Not a lot of hair for people to get into," he said. "We'll question the cast first to free them up to do their show. Anything else?"

"Not at the moment."

"Okay. By the way, where were you when he was shot?"

"Me? I was sitting in the audience along with everyone else."

"Did you know the deceased?"

"No. I'd never met him before arriving here for

the weekend. Actually, we were never really introduced. I saw him in the play during rehearsal and bumped into him earlier this evening."

"Where was that?"

"Just inside the rear door downstairs. It seems to be a place where smokers go to have a cigarette."

"Show it to me?"

"Certainly."

I led him to the area, where cigarette butts still littered the floor. A uniformed officer was posted to ensure that no one left the premises.

"I came through this door after taking a walk," I said, "and Paul—the deceased—was standing here smoking a cigarette."

"You talk to him?"

"Just barely. I was startled to see him here, and said so. He snuffed out his cigarette and left"—I pointed—"up those stairs. The next time I saw him was during the first act this evening. He left the stage with the young actress. There was the shot. She raced into the room screaming, as she was supposed to do according to the script, and he stumbled back onto the set, pretending to have been shot. But as we know, he wasn't pretending."

The detective pushed a few butts with the toe of his boot and looked around the small space. "Who's the murderer in the play?" he asked absently.

"In the play? I don't know. I haven't seen it before. It's a new show. The Savoys are putting it on for the first time this weekend."

"Do me a favor and take a look at the script," he

said. "I have to get back. Thanks for your cooperation."

I followed him up to the main floor and decided
to go to my room. I was standing at the elevator
when Larry Savoy approached. "The detective has
agreed to let you continue with the show," I said.
"So has Mark Egmon, although he has to get final
management approval." The elevator doors opened,
but I pulled Larry aside. "Larry," I said in a low
voice, "do you have any hunches about who might
have killed Paul?"

He shrugged.

"If it was a member of the cast, is there one person
who might have had it in for him?"

He chewed his cheek and frowned. "No, Jess, but
I really hadn't thought about it before. He wasn't the
most popular guy with the cast and crew. Arrogance
was his middle name." He lowered his voice. "Do
you really think the killer is a cast member?"

"I have no idea," I said. "But someone shot Paul
backstage, and unless one of the guests came here
with the intention of killing him, considering cast
members as primary suspects seems logical."

"I suppose you're right. Look, I'm assembling the
cast on the enclosed front porch in half an hour. Join
us? With your track record for solving murders, I'd
feel better having you around. I've invited the other
writers, too."

"Of course I'll be there," I said. "Count on it. Oh,
Detective Ladd has asked me to read the script. He

wants to see who the murderer is in the show with a thought to linking it up with what really happened."

"I could tell you, but I won't. I'll get you a script, but I can't see anything coming of it."

"I agree," I said, "but I said I would look. Thanks."

He walked away, and I pressed the button for the elevator again. But instead of getting in when it arrived, I descended the stairs and returned to the unofficial smoking area just inside the lower door. I pulled a Kleenex from my pocket and used it to push the discarded cigarette butts into a neat pile, which I carefully picked up with the tissue. That chore completed, I went to my room. The cigarette butts I'd collected from the balcony were still in the trash. I retrieved them from the wastebasket, spread everything out on a sheet of paper, and examined them. I knew nothing about the slain actor, but was looking for anything that would link another person to him. Had his killer shared a cigarette with him prior to pulling the trigger? Probably not. But at least I'd taken a first action. And as my doctor friend, Seth Hazlitt, back in Cabot Cove always says, any action is better than no action.

Chapter Nine

John Dickson Carr specialized in a certain type of murder mystery plot. What was it?

It wasn't late enough for bed, and after what had just occurred I was too wound up to settle into the mundane pleasure of reading a book. I left my room and wandered down to a small lounge that housed Mohawk House's only bar, whimsically named Earl's Pub. As I approached the room, I could hear a pianist and accompanying musicians playing one of my favorite tunes, "Cheek to Cheek."

I stood in the doorway and took in my surroundings. I'd assumed that the events of the evening would cast a somber pall over the guests, even though most of them probably weren't sure whether what had occurred on the stage was real or part of the production. I had thought the presence of uniformed police throughout the building, and the fact that no one was allowed to leave, would have injected a hefty dose of reality into the situation. But that didn't seem to be the case.

The bar was busy and festive despite two dour cops in uniform watching over the gathering, one stationed at each of the two doors. Couples danced to the trio's infectious beat while others gathered in small groups, drinks in hand and voices raised— badly, I might add—as they sang the words to the familiar melodies cranked out by the pianist, an older black woman, and her colleagues, a bassist and drummer. Considering what I knew to have happened, the scene was surreal, something out of an avant-garde movie. A young man had been shot to death in front of a hundred witnesses, and a party was in full swing.

I was debating leaving when a male voice close behind me said, "Buy you a drink?" It was John Chasseur.

"I hadn't planned on staying," I said.

"Come on, be a sport," he said. "I hate to drink alone."

We went to a spot at the bar where two adjacent barstools were vacant. When we'd settled on them, he asked, "And what does the famous Jessica Fletcher drink?"

"That depends," I replied. "Right now, a tall glass of orange juice sounds perfect."

"Orange juice is for breakfast," he said.

"Back home in Maine," I said, "orange juice is considered a proper drink at any time of the day."

"The lady will have an orange juice, straight up," he told the bartender. "A perfect Manhattan for me, no cherry." He turned to me and asked, "So, have you got it all figured out yet?"

"Afraid not. You?"

"Sure I do. Paul, our dead actor, probably did dirt to some pretty young thing, maybe somebody's wife, and she whacked him."

"You make it sound like a mob hit."

"Iced him. Offed him. It's all the same."

"Why do you assume it was a woman who shot him?"

He shrugged and sipped his drink. "Makes sense, doesn't it? Handsome kid like that must have had plenty of broads falling all over him. Hard to figure women. It's all surface with them. The kid probably had the mind of a mole and was a quarter inch deep, but he looked good. That's all that seems to count with the so-called fairer sex, present company excepted, of course."

I had no interest in getting into a debate with an obvious misogynist, so I took a long swallow of my juice and said nothing.

"Offended?" he said.

"Not at all," I said. "I do feel a little sorry, though."

"For what?"

"For you."

He guffawed. "Don't waste your sorrow on me, Jessica Fletcher. I'm at the top of my game, on the upside."

"Are you inferring that my career is on a downward slope?"

"No. Touchy, are we?"

"Sometimes."

"Okay, so maybe I am a little hard on women,"

he said. "Maybe it wasn't a woman who killed the actor." He snickered. "Maybe it was the ghost of Mohawk House, the headless earl."

"Believe in ghosts?" I asked, taking another taste of my drink.

"Ghosts? Sure. Why not? Hollywood's filled with them. Real ones. And ghouls, too."

"How many of your books have been made into motion pictures?" I asked.

"I've had half a dozen optioned, but only two have made it to the screen. I'm producing now. Writers are treated like dirt in Hollywood. All the real action is in producing."

"Have I seen any films you've produced?" I asked.

"Maybe, maybe not. I've been doing low-budget ones as a start, but I've got some major projects in development. Maybe one of your books would make a good flick."

"Perhaps." I didn't bother mentioning that some of my novels had been optioned and were the basis for motion pictures. "Where's your wife?" I asked.

"In the room fussing with her hair or something. Actresses are all alike, vain as all get-out and looking for the secret to eternal youth."

"She's an actress?"

"Not a very successful one. A couple of grade-B films. I rescued her."

Judging from the way he'd treated her at dinner, he hadn't done her any favors by "rescuing" her.

"She's a beautiful woman," I said. "How long have you been married?"

He started to answer when Detective Ladd entered the room and came to us. "Enjoying yourselves?" he asked, his eyes going from table to table.

"I'm not sure that's the way I'd characterize it," I said, "but a break certainly is welcome. Anything new in your investigation?"

He shook his head, his attention still on others in the room.

"Mr. Chasseur has a theory about who killed the actor," I said.

"Is that so, Mr. Chasseur?" Ladd said. "I'd love to hear it."

Chasseur shot me a nasty look. I smiled. He said, "I think I'd better be going." He stood, laid a twenty-dollar bill on the bar, and said, "Have a good evening."

When he was gone, Ladd took his place at the bar. "What's this theory of his?" he asked.

"Ignore what I said, Detective. I was making a point with him."

He ordered a club soda from the bartender. "The ME got the body out of here just in time," he said. "Another couple of inches of snow and our departed actor would have been with us for the duration." He leaned close to me and said, "I understand you're pretty tight with the Savoys."

"Oh, I wouldn't say that," I replied. "We've appeared together before, but I don't see much of them socially."

"What about the actors and actresses?"

"All strangers to me until this weekend. Why do you ask?"

"Just trying to get a handle on the players."

"The suspects."

"Yeah, the suspects. What about the young gal, Laura Tehaar, the one who was supposed to shoot off the phony gun?"

"I know nothing about her," I said.

"What about the victim?"

"As I told you, I bumped into him—literally—only today, and saw him during a rehearsal."

Ladd nodded, swiveled on his stool, and scrutinized the crowd, which had begun to thin out. He returned his attention to me. "Can you keep a secret?" he asked.

"I believe I can, but be warned, Detective. Secrets have a way of not staying secret once they've been told to another person, no matter how closemouthed that other person might be." He started to respond, but I interrupted with, "Might I ask why you would trust me with a secret? It obviously has to do with the murder that has taken place here this evening. I'm just another witness, another suspect."

"From what I'm told, Mrs. Fletcher, you're a lot more than that. Not only do you write murder mysteries, but you've also solved your share of real ones. Am I right?"

"That has happened on occasion."

"So, I figure I can use all the help I can get with this one."

"I'm flattered, of course, and will do anything I can to help."

His lips almost touched my ear as he whispered, "The deceased wasn't shot."

There was no need for me to respond verbally. My face said it all.

"That's right," he whispered again. "He wasn't shot."

"But—"

"He was stabbed. Everybody assumed he was shot because of the sound of gunfire off the stage. But the ME says it was a knife wound that killed him. The gunshot sound must have been from the pistol with blanks that Ms. Tehaar fired."

"I see," I said.

"So, do me a favor, Mrs. Fletcher."

"Of course."

"Keep your eyes open for somebody carrying a bloody knife. And keep this to yourself, okay?"

My mind raced. The news that a knife had been used to kill Paul Brody changed, to some extent, the perception of what sort of individual might have killed him. A woman is less likely to use a knife as a murder weapon than a man. A knife is up close and personal. A gun is less so. That isn't to say that plenty of women haven't used knives to kill someone, nor should a woman ever be ruled out as a suspect simply on the basis of that premise. But statistically, a betting person would be safer placing a bet on a man using a knife to kill someone.

Two women carrying notebooks interrupted us.

"Excuse me," one of them said to Detective Ladd. "I hate to bother you, but we were told it was all right to approach any of the actors at any time during the weekend."

Ladd's expression was one of confusion. He looked at me. If he was seeking my help, he was disappointed. All I could do was smile. Like many others in the hotel that weekend, these women obviously had decided that a real murder had *not* taken place, and that this real police officer was part of the cast. Ladd picked up on what was happening and said, "Sorry, but as long as the investigation is continuing, I'm not at liberty to discuss it."

"Oh, that isn't fair," said the second woman. With pen poised over her notepad, she said, "Now, I believe that the maid should be looked at very, v-e-r-y closely. Have you interrogated her, Detective?"

"I, ah—I haven't gotten around to it yet," Ladd said, "but you're correct. I'll question—I'll *interrogate* her right now. Excuse me."

He left me with the two amateur sleuths. One said, "Mrs. Fletcher, maybe you can help straighten something out for me. There seem to be two officers in charge of the investigation." She consulted her notes. "There's Detective Carboroni, and now this detective. We don't even have his name."

"His name is—" I stopped, assuming that Ladd would be just as happy not having his name bandied about. "I think he might announce it at the next performance. Then again, he might prefer to operate incognito."

"Oh, yes, of course," one of the women said. "I hadn't thought of that."

"Well," said her friend, "I'm just glad someone like you is here to keep an eye on things. You won't mind, will you, if we stay close?"

"Of course not. It will be my pleasure."

I excused myself and left the room with the intention of going to my suite and calling it a night. I was on my way to the elevators when Victoria, the actress playing Mrs. Whittaker in the play, approached.

"Good evening," I said.

"Hello," she said. "I still can't believe what happened to Paul."

"I know. It was so sudden, so tragic. A young life snuffed out like that."

"Not such a young life," she said.

"Pardon?"

"Paul wasn't as young as he looked. I liked to kid him about being too old to play juvenile leads."

"How old was he?" I asked.

"Late thirties."

"He certainly didn't look it," I said. "I would have thought early twenties."

"He didn't act his age, either. You'd think those dismal years in Hollywood would have matured him."

The elevator arrived.

"Coming to the cast meeting?" Victoria asked.

"Oh, my goodness, I forgot about that. Larry asked me to attend. I'm glad I bumped into you."

As we walked together to an enclosed porch where

the cast had gathered, the things I'd just learned whirled in my brain, and I was anxious to get to my room where I could start making notes of my own. There were two murders to solve that weekend, the one written into the script and the one that had occurred earlier in the evening. I hoped there wouldn't be a third—theatrical *or* real.

Chapter Ten

The first Shamus Awards were presented at Bouchercon in San Francisco in 1982. What genre of crime writing do the awards honor?

A uniformed officer stationed at the door to the enclosed porch stopped us as we tried to enter. "This is a private meeting," he said.

"And we're part of it," Victoria said.

Larry Savoy saw through the glass doors what was happening and came to us. "They're part of the group," he told the officer, who grunted and stepped aside to allow us to enter.

"Sorry I'm late," I said as we followed Larry to a couple of empty chairs at the front.

"It's okay," he said. "I'm just glad you're here. Some of the troupe have second thoughts about continuing."

Our arrival didn't hush those already in attendance. A spirited argument was under way, with everyone talking at once. Some voices were loud, and an occasional four-letter word cut through the general din. Monroe suddenly rose from his chair and took center stage. Wearing a fresh smoking jacket like the one that had been used to cover Paul Brody's body, he stepped in front of Savoy. With his hands on his hips, he looked very much as though he was playing the father's role again. He raised his hands in a plea for silence and said in a booming voice, "Please, pay attention to what I have to say."

No one heeded him, so he repeated it, louder this time. A few ceased talking, and eventually the noise level lowered to the point where Whittaker could be heard. "I feel as though I'm surrounded by babies," he said in the stentorian tones of a veteran stage actor. "Do none of you have any respect for what has come before you, the traditions of the theater, the giants who have walked the great stages of the world, the men and women who treasured the age-old tradition of the show having to go on no matter what tragedies intrude?"

"Oh, can it, Monroe," someone said.

Whittaker's expression was one of abject hurt. Larry Savoy came around in front of him and said to the cast, "The least we can do is hear what Monroe has to say, and respect his right to say it."

Cynthia stood and faced her acting colleagues. Fighting back tears, she said, "I don't like going through with it any more than you do, but I'm willing to do so. After all, Paul fell dead at my feet, not yours. His blood is on my shoe, not yours. Monroe is right. We all have to grow up and respect tradition."

Melinda Savoy stood as Cynthia sat. "You might keep in mind," she said, "that none of us are going anywhere while the police investigate Paul's murder. We have a choice. Either we sit in our rooms and feel sorry for ourselves, or you perform for those people who paid good money to see our play. Besides, unless you came here by dogsled, you aren't going anyplace until the storm stops." She looked at me and said, "You won't find Mrs. Fletcher or the other writers running away from their commitments."

The cast's eyes turned to me. I nodded my agreement with what Melinda had said. As I did, loud voices outside the doors captured everyone's attention. I saw through the glass that John Chasseur and GSB Wick were arguing with the officer. Larry started for the door, but I stood and told him I'd take care of it.

Chasseur was chastising the officer for his arrogance. When he saw me, he demanded, "What is this, some sort of plot to keep us out?"

"Not at all," I said. I told the officer, "These people are part of the program this weekend. They should be attending the meeting."

He reluctantly granted them access to the porch. As we reentered, Laura Tehaar, the young woman in charge of props, pushed past us in the direction of the door. She stopped, turned, and with tears streaming down her cheeks, she shouted, "All you care about are your own needs and feelings. Paul is dead! Murdered! I hate all of you!" With that, she was gone.

"Emotional little thing, isn't she?" Chasseur said as he and Georgie Wick found seats. A cast member had taken the chair next to Victoria that I'd vacated, so I joined my writing colleagues.

"So, what have we missed, Jessica?" Chasseur asked.

"They're debating whether to continue with the play."

"I didn't mean them," he said. "I meant with the investigation. You seemed wired in with that hick cop. Has he solved the murder yet?"

I ignored the snide question and said, "Detective Ladd strikes me as a capable young man. I'm sure he's doing his best to get to the bottom of things."

"I wouldn't dare write him into a novel," he said. "He looks like he'd be more at home tending to cows and pigs."

Larry Savoy managed to quiet the crowd again and said, "Okay, let's do it this way. Some of you have indicated to me privately that you're willing to continue with the show, but now that you're all here, let's put it to a vote. All in favor of going on with the show raise your hands."

I counted, along with Larry. Only a few failed to respond favorably.

"All right," he said. "We keep going."

One of those who hadn't raised his hand said, "Just because the majority wants to continue, it doesn't mean I have to."

"That's true," said Larry. "But like Melinda said, you can't leave the hotel anyway. You might as well keep busy working on the production. Besides, if you don't work, you don't get paid."

"Tell that to the union," the man retorted.

"I'll be happy to," Larry said. "Okay, let's get some rehearsal in. See you in fifteen minutes in the auditorium."

The cast and crew filed out, leaving Larry and Melinda Savoy, Chasseur, GSB Wick, and me on the porch. "Well," Larry said, "looks like we keep on going. I hope that includes the three of you."

"I'm willing," Chasseur said, "but I do have an objection to lodge."

"Which is?"

"It seems that Jessica here has been given some special access to what's going on."

"That's not true," I said.

"It doesn't matter what you say, Jessica. It's the facts that count. Ms. Wick and I aren't told of things like this meeting, Larry's plans, and what progress the bumpkin detective is making. I insist on being informed of such things."

"I assure you no one has decided to cut you, or anyone else, out, John," Melinda assured him.

"I'll take your word for it, Melinda," Chasseur said. "Let's just make sure it stays that way."

Chasseur seemed appeased, at least for the moment. My dilemma, I realized, was that I didn't have any control over the extent to which Detective Ladd chose to confide in me and not the others. Now that I knew that Paul Brody had been stabbed, not shot, did I have an obligation to share that information with my fellow writers? I thought not, and hoped that my being in possession of such inside information could be kept from them.

Larry asked whether we wanted to attend the rehearsal. Chasseur said he did; Ms. Wick and I declined the invitation. She and I left the porch together and walked slowly in the direction of the lobby and elevators.

"I would very much like a nightcap," she said. "Will you join me?"

"I'm glad to see that you're feeling better," I said.

"Just a case of nerves," she replied.

We went to the bar where I'd been earlier and took a booth in a far corner. There weren't as many people there as had been previously. The trio was packing up their instruments, and it looked like the bartender was getting ready to call it a night. He spotted us. "Last call," he announced pleasantly.

After Wick had ordered what seemed to be her usual—a Bacardi cocktail—and I'd opted for a tall glass of cold water, she said, "Well, well, well, here we are cooped up for the weekend with a murderer."

"Frankly," I said, "I hope that we are."

She looked at me and frowned. "Whatever do you mean by *that*?"

I laughed. "If we are, cooped up with the murderer," I said, "it means that whoever killed Paul is still here. If the killer managed to flee, he, or she, might never be found."

"Frankly, that wouldn't bother me a bit," she said as our drinks were placed before us and I signed for them using my room number. She took a sip, smacked her thin lips, and said, "Now I'm really feeling better."

"Mind a question?" I asked.

"Not at all, but if it's about Harold, I plead no contest."

"No," I said, "it's not about your friend. I was wondering—"

"Harold says he finds you very attractive."

"Oh? That's flattering."

"Don't mind him. He can be a bit of a lecher, I know. All those years alone with dead bodies, I suppose."

"Yes, I suppose. I was wondering what to call you."

"Call me?"

"Yes."

"Oh, you mean what name to use."

"Exactly."

"Georgie is fine."

"Mind another question?"

"No."

"What do your other initials stand for, the *S* and the *B*?"

She grinned impishly and took a long sip of her cocktail. "I'm afraid I prefer to keep that little secret to myself," she said, more to the glass than to me.

"As you wish," I said. If it was important for her to maintain a veil of secrecy about it, so be it.

"Maybe the slain earl's murderer has struck again," she offered absently.

I smiled and said, "Actually, that would be preferable. I'd prefer a ghostly killer to a flesh-and-blood one."

Her face became animated. "As would I," she said as though my comment had opened a floodgate of thoughts within her. "So many people are cynical when it comes to ghosts, Jessica. I'm not one of them. Are you?"

"I suppose my view is that I have no reason *not* to believe in them. Like extraterrestrial creatures. I doubt if they're there, but since I really don't *know* whether they are or not, I have to assume they could be."

She said nothing, as though pondering the mysteries of the universe. I took the moment to look at her more closely. The conversation about ghosts seemed apt. GSB Wick had a "ghostly" quality about her, a not-of-this-world aura—the milky white skin stretched tight over her cheekbones, the bloodred lipstick that made her mouth seem larger than it really was, the raven hair and slightly garish green eye shadow with its tiny sparkles above small, piercing black eyes that seemed to focus on something only she could see.

"Once ah had a lover who looked very much like the young man slain here tonight," she said, her Southern accent deepening, making her sound like Blanche DuBois in *A Streetcar Named Desire*.

"Oh?"

"Yes, a fine, handsome young man with a wonderful future in the theater."

I wasn't sure what to say next, so I said nothing.

"We were very much in love until—"

She paused. Was she about to cry? I had the distinct feeling that she now was gazing into some private world unavailable to me, or anyone else for that matter.

"Until he was cut down in the prime of his youth." Her expression brightened. "Oh, mah, what a splendid boy he was. When he comes to visit, he always brings me flowers and says the sweetest things."

"I, um—"

She sensed my discomfort, turned to face me, and said, "Ah imagine you think I'm strange, Jessica."

"Oh, no," I said. "As I mentioned before, I don't dismiss any possibilities in this world, not when I don't have facts to back me up." I conspicuously looked at my watch. "I think it's time for this lady to call it a night."

Her response was to wave the young bartender over to the booth. When he arrived she said, "Ah would be much obliged if you would make me one more of these heavenly drinks."

"Sorry, ma'am, but I'm closed."

She placed a bony hand on his, smiled sweetly, and said, "Considerin' what's happened here this evening, certainly you can make an exception for a lonely old woman."

He looked to me. I smiled and said, "It would be a true act of kindness."

He nodded, smiled, and said to Georgie, "One Bacardi cocktail coming up."

Chapter Eleven

A certain era is considered to be the "Golden Age" of murder mysteries. Was it the 1920s through the 1940s? The 1950s until the late 1970s? Or the 1980s through the mid-1990s?

I was happy to get to my room, kick off my shoes, and reflect on what had transpired that day. I sat at a small desk in the corner, pulled a sheet of hotel stationery from the drawer, and began to make notes. I'd just gotten started when the phone rang.

"Hello?"

"Mrs. Fletcher, this is Detective Ladd. Hope I didn't wake you."

"No, not at all. I just got here."

"Got a few minutes?"

"Of course."

"Meet you downstairs? Mr. Egmon has given me a private room to use."

"Fine."

He was there when I arrived. "Have a seat," he said. "Anybody from the press try to reach you tonight?"

"The press? No. Why do you ask?"

He twisted his torso against a pain in his neck or

back, winced, and shook his head. "This is a funny town, Mrs. Fletcher. The leaders like to keep everything hush-hush, if you know what I mean."

"Like a murder in its midst?" I said.

"You've got it," he said. "Especially since it happened here at Mohawk House."

"Why would that make a difference?"

"Clout. Seems like nine-tenths of the people in the town work here. The mayor, my boss, called me and said I was to keep it under wraps until things got resolved. As far as he's concerned, having a murder splashed all over the newspapers and on the tube would be bad for business."

I couldn't help but smile, and thought that as far as murder mystery weekends went, having a real killing take place would add to their appeal, certainly to mystery buffs. But I didn't challenge him. Instead, I asked, "Why are you telling me this?"

"Because you seem to be the biggest name here this weekend. The way I figure it, if the press wants to find out what's going on at the hotel, they'll be looking to interview someone like you."

I started to protest his logic but he cut me off.

"Makes sense, doesn't it? Get a famous mystery writer to give her impressions of what happened."

I started to say something again, but he held up his hand. "Look, Mrs. Fletcher, I know that you can say and do anything you please. All I'm asking is that you consider keeping mum for a while. Not only that, but I have a feeling that you carry some weight with the others, the actors and actresses, the writers who are here with you, that sort of thing."

I thought for a moment before saying, "I'll be happy to avoid making statements to anyone outside the hotel, and I'll do my best to convey your message to the Savoys, the cast, and the writers. But I can't promise anything."

"Sure, I know that."

"I must say, though, that confiding in me about aspects of the murder places me in somewhat of an awkward position."

"How so?"

I explained that some of the others were envious of what they perceived as my special treatment.

"You mean Mr. Chasseur."

"For one."

"He's not my favorite guy, Mrs. Fletcher. I hear he's been going around saying nasty things about me and my handling of this case."

I didn't respond.

"And that actor who plays the cop in the play, Carboroni? Turns out he used to be a cop in Philadelphia. He's like my shadow, acting like he's still the real thing."

"Well," I said, "I'm sure you're used to dealing with difficult people. Have you questioned many of the guests yet?"

"Not as many as I'd like to, but I'll get around to it. That Mrs. Wick"—he chuckled and shook his head—"she's a real character, isn't she?"

"She's, ah—she's different."

"That's what I meant, only you put it nicer. By the way, Mrs. Fletcher, what do you know about the deceased's history, family, that sort of thing?"

"Absolutely nothing, I'm afraid." I remembered what Victoria had said about Paul Brody being older than he looked, and mentioned that to Ladd, who noted it on a small notepad. "And he evidently spent time in Hollywood," I added, "at least according to Victoria, the actress who plays the mother in the show, and Larry Savoy."

"Mr. Savoy is getting me information so we can notify his next-of-kin. Not my favorite job, let me tell you."

"I would think not," I said. "Well, are we finished?"

"For now. I just want you to know how much I appreciate your cooperation, Mrs. Fletcher."

"I'm only too happy to help."

"Yeah," he said, walking me to the door, "I need all the help I can get, this being my first murder investigation."

Chapter Twelve

Clint Eastwood starred in the film version of
Firefox, *penned by a leading British thriller writer.*
Who is he?

I felt for the young lawman as I watched him walk away. His first murder investigation certainly wasn't going to be easy, no matter how much help he might receive.

I admired his honesty. Many macho policemen wouldn't have admitted to being a novice, particularly to a woman who'd injected herself into their business from the start. Until Detective Ladd's revelation that he'd never investigated a homicide, I'd found myself anxious to get to the bottom of who'd killed Paul Brody. That's my nature, I suppose, built into the genes. But now I had an even greater incentive, and I wanted to do everything I could to aid Detective Ladd.

I considered dropping by the late-night rehearsal that was now under way but decided instead to explore portions of Mohawk House I hadn't seen yet. As I passed the main check-in desk, one of the staff on duty, an older man, stopped me.

"Anything I can do for you?" he asked.

"Thank you, no," I said. "Just taking a self-conducted tour of this grand old lady of a building."

He laughed. "We're just hoping this grand old lady will weather the storm."

"Have you heard the latest forecast?" I asked.

"Sure have. They keep upping the snowfall totals. They're calling it the worst March storm in the area's history. Could be up to four feet, they say."

"Oh, my," I said. "How unfortunate for the guests this weekend."

He motioned me closer to the desk. "You're Mrs. Fletcher," he said in a low voice.

"Yes."

He looked past me to where two uniformed officers stood just inside the front door. He lowered his voice even more and asked, "Is it true that one of the actors was murdered? I mean *really* murdered?"

"I'm not sure what happened," I said. "There was an accident and—"

"I heard he was murdered," he said with conviction.

"Until the police decide to release information," I said, "it's probably best for everyone to go about their business and try not to speculate."

He glanced over at a young colleague who was busy doing paperwork at the opposite end of the long desk. "Lorraine says she thinks the killer is still here. She and some of the others wanted to leave, but the snow made it impossible. You can't make it down the mountain in this weather. You'll end up dead just like him, if he's really dead. I can't believe it was Mr. Brody."

" 'Mr. Brody'? You sound as though you knew him."

"Oh, yes. Not well, but he used to come here with his family."

"How long ago?" I asked.

"Oh, years and years ago. Little scamps, those boys were, that's for sure, always running around, playing make-believe, that sort of thing. His brother's name was Peter. I remember that because whenever I saw them together, I thought of having to rob Peter to pay Paul." He chuckled. "You could tell they were from a theatrical family. Lots of imagination. They loved finding secret places in the building—and believe me, we have plenty of those." He shook his head, smiling. "I remember one time they got stuck in an abandoned stairwell and started screaming for help. They'd found their way there, but couldn't figure out how to get back."

"You said it was a theatrical family. What did the parents do?"

"The father was a producer. Theater, I believe, more than motion pictures, although I think he was involved in that, too. Very wealthy guy, made his money in pharmaceuticals, I think. The mother had been a showgirl. Nice-looking woman."

"Did you speak with the son this weekend?" I asked.

"Oh yes, had a brief chat with him. Very brief. I said

I remembered him from when the family vacationed here, and when he'd spent a summer in the area."

"When was that?" I asked.

"Not exactly certain." He scratched his head. "The brain doesn't remember as well as it used to."

"You remembered Paul Brody and his family coming to Mohawk House."

"Well, that's going back some. The newer stuff doesn't stick with me so well. But I remember he was here, appeared in a summer stock production in a small theater, the Newsome, on the other side of town. Turned into a movie house now. Must've been about a dozen years ago."

"That the theater became a movie house?"

"No, no. That young Paul was acting there. Didn't pay much; he worked odd jobs to bring in some extra money. I thought he might come to work here but he didn't. Sad."

"Sad that he didn't come to work here?"

"No. I was disappointed that he didn't seem to have much of a recollection of it. He said he vaguely remembered coming here as a youngster with his folks, but told me he'd never been here working in summer stock. Made me feel foolish. Oh, well. I'm sorry that he's gone, and in such a terrible way. All I can say, Mrs. Fletcher, is that if what I'm hearing is true, there are going to be a lot of upset people around here."

"It's natural for nerves to be a little frayed," I said, "but I'm sure everyone will be fine. The biggest problem seems to be what Mother Nature has decided to dump on us. I think I'll take a look around myself. I enjoyed our chat.''

''Me, too. It's fun reminiscing about old times. You know, I was in the theater once myself. Did some acting as a young man but got smart and took up something with a steady paycheck. I've been here many, many years and wouldn't trade it for any other job. I really enjoy working the desk, welcoming guests, seeing to it that they're happy. I meet lots of interesting people—like you and Mr. Brody. The father, I mean. The boys, too.'' He grinned. ''And of course there was the accountants' convention. You think those guys are serious, but you get them all together and they play pranks on each other, just like kids. I could tell you some things. Give you lots of material for your books, I bet.'' He paused, and a flush rose to his cheeks. ''I hope you'll excuse me, Mrs. Fletcher. I can go on and on. The boss thinks I talk too much, take up too much of the guests' time. But when you work in a hotel, there's no end to the stories. It's late. I'm sorry I kept you.''

''Don't trouble yourself about it at all. You didn't keep me, and I'm sure we'll have a chance to talk again.'' I gave him a little wave as I turned back toward the hall.

I went to the glass doors where two uniformed officers stood watch. The storm was raging, the snow blowing horizontally to create a white sheet that obscured everything beyond.

"I've seen bad snowstorms before where I come from," I said to the officers, "but nothing as fast-moving as this."

"Worst in history," said one. "The mayor's declared a state of emergency."

"Well," I said, "we're fortunate to be in this warm building."

"As long as we don't lose electricity," said the second officer.

"I certainly hope we don't," I said.

I bid them good night and continued my exploration of Mohawk House, going down a hallway I hadn't seen before. It led to a small circular room that jutted out from one corner of the building. Large windows that afforded a ringside seat for the storm rattled in the wind. Two high-backed, overstuffed chairs flanked a small table and a single low-wattage lamp cast a small pool of yellow light in the room. I thought I was alone. But as I was about to leave, I sensed that someone was seated in one of the chairs. I took a few steps into the space and saw that it was Claudette Chasseur. She sat perfectly still, her head listing slightly to one side, eyes cast down. Was she sleeping? I wondered, or—?

I fabricated a cough. No movement. I tried again, a little louder this time. She stirred, bringing her head up straight, and turned slightly in my direction.

All I could see was her elegant profile. She had delicate features and her skin was pale and translucent, the veins of her cheek a pale shadow beneath the fine surface.

"It's quite a storm," I said. "You've found the perfect spot from which to watch it."

"I wasn't watching," she said.

I hesitated before asking, "Mind if I join you?"

"Suit yourself."

I took the other chair. She remained in the same position as when I'd arrived, one long leg crossed over the other, torso erect, her eyes open but focused on her hands, which lay in her lap. She gripped a tissue in one tightly curled fist.

"They say this will be the worst storm in history for this area," I said, trying to make conversation.

"I hate it," she said.

I smiled. "I can understand someone from sunny California not liking cold and snow. I guess I'm used to it. We have very rugged winters in Maine. That's where I live. To us, that's the way the season is supposed to be. It makes us appreciate spring that much more when it finally arrives."

"I guess you would," she said, raising her eyes and staring blankly at the windows and the wintry show playing out beyond them.

"Has your husband gone to bed?" I asked, wondering whether the lady preferred to be alone and not engage in conversation.

"I suppose," she said.

Now she turned to face me. The area surrounding her left eye was swollen and discolored, and her streaked makeup indicated she'd been crying.

"That's a nasty-looking bruise," I said. "Did you fall?"

"Fall?" she repeated, punctuating the word with a cynical chortle. "Try walking into a line of knuckles." She turned away from me again, her mouth set in a hard, straight line. I knew I shouldn't press for more information, but I wasn't comfortable saying nothing. I decided to be direct.

"Did your husband do that to you?" I asked, certain that I already knew the answer.

She nodded, gently placed the fingertips of her left hand on the bruise, and drew in a sharp breath. "It's bad, isn't it?"

"Maybe you should see a doctor," I suggested. "I'm sure the hotel has one on call."

"And I'm sure he can't wait to come out in a blizzard to patch up my eye."

She had a point.

"Do you mind if I ask whether your husband has hit you before?"

"You can ask anything you want," she said. "Has he hit me before? Yes. How many times? A few. Why do I put up with it? Because right now he's all I've got."

"*All you've got?*" I said, incredulous. "You're young and beautiful and have your whole life ahead of you. Why would you have such a low opinion of yourself?"

She faced me. "Ever tried to make it in Hollywood as an actress, Mrs. Fletcher?"

"It's Jessica. And no, I can't say that I've ever had any aspirations to act."

"Women who look like me—some far more beautiful—are a dime a dozen in Hollywood. I think I have talent, but no one was interested in finding out if it's true. I was just one of many young women who win a local beauty pageant and leave their hometowns to become Hollywood stars. I roomed with three of them. We used to tell each other we were going to become, you know, *overnight sensations*, living in a Beverly Hills mansion, walking down the red carpet at the Academy Awards dressed in designer clothes, the hunks of the week on our arms. But it doesn't take you long to realize that those dreams are just that, naïve dreams that have as much chance of coming true as wanting to become an astronaut. At least I didn't end up on the street—or worse."

She'd become emotional as she spoke, animated and earnest. I didn't want to interrupt the flow, so I said nothing, content to be a sincerely interested listener. Besides, she didn't need any prompting from me to continue.

"You start getting down on yourself," she said. "You're embarrassed that you've failed, and you dread ever going home again where they know you headed to Hollywood to be a star. 'Some star!' they would think, and be secretly glad you fell on your face because they never liked you in high school and are happy that you didn't make it. They didn't make it either, of course, but they never promised they would. That's the difference."

"It seems to me that I heard you had some success in Hollywood," I said. "Didn't you appear in some films?"

Her laugh was rueful. "None that you've ever seen, I'm sure, Jessica. There's always a part in porn flicks. I did my share of them, not hard-core but soft porn, nothing I wanted to write home to my folks about. Thank God they'll never see them. They would never watch garbage like that. And there was John's film. That was the last role I ever had."

"You mean your husband, John Chasseur?"

"Uh-huh. An independent producer bought the rights to one of his books. Part of John's deal was that he'd be listed as a producer, one of a dozen. That was okay with him because he always wanted to live and work in Hollywood, play the big shot, live the Hollywood high life. So he got to do some casting for the film. A girlfriend of mine knew where they were holding the readings. We bought the book, dressed up the way we thought the character would, went to the studio, and charmed our way past the security guard. There must have been a hundred other girls there who'd done the same thing. My friend was sent home, but I was asked to stay. I met John." She hesitated. "And got the part." She held her hand up to me. "And, yes, Jessica, it was a classic casting couch situation. John was between marriages and needed somebody on his arm, somebody to feed his ego and pick up his dry cleaning. He proposed, I said yes, and here we are."

"It doesn't sound like a match made in heaven," I said.

"You might say that. But as I said, it's all I have. The folks back home—that's a little town outside St. Louis—they think I married a big-shot movie producer and writer, so to them it looks like maybe I did succeed. Pathetic, huh?"

"Certainly sad," I said. "I think you're selling yourself short. You're obviously a bright woman along with your good looks. What's most important is that you not allow John, or anyone for that matter, to abuse you. He has no right to lay a hand on you for any reason. You must do something to put a stop to it, even if it means leaving him."

"Oh, don't think I haven't considered that every day, Jessica. But I—"

Her eyes filled, and she began to weep softly. I placed my hand on her arm and squeezed. "Would you like to stay in my room tonight?" I asked. "There are two queen-sized beds. It wouldn't be an imposition."

"No, but thank you," she said, pulling another tissue from a pocket and dabbing at her eyes. "I'd better get back."

"Did you have much of a part in your husband's motion picture?" I asked.

"Not a lead or anything, but I had some lines and a pretty good scene with the male lead."

"I'd love to see it," I said. "Is it out on video or DVD?"

"Yes, it is."

"What's the title?"

"*Murder by Special Delivery.*"

"I'll look for it."

I gave her my room number in case she changed her mind, and watched her walk slowly away, straightening and stiffening as though girding for something distinctly unpleasant. *Poor thing*, I thought, *so typical of too many women who have options but fail to see and act upon them.* I was deep in that thought when, behind me, the loud sound of shattering glass caused me to jump. I spun around to see that a sizable tree limb, carried by the wind, had smashed one of the windows, and a torrent of frigid air and snow poured through the gaping hole. Almost immediately, a maintenance man who'd been working in the area appeared.

"Are you all right, ma'am?" he asked.

"Yes, thank you, I'm fine," I said, wrapping my arms about me against the windy chill.

He ran up the hall in search of something to repair the damage, and I went in the opposite direction, happy to get away from the storm's intrusion into the hotel's inner recesses.

I went to my room, where I changed into nightclothes and the terry-cloth robe, performed my usual bedtime ablutions, and resumed making notes. Although I'd been wide awake all evening, it was late and the warmth from the fire made me drowsy. I left the light on in the bathroom, which I always do to ensure that I won't trip over something on my way there in the middle of the night, left the bathroom door slightly ajar, and climbed into bed. I fell asleep immediately, but awoke two hours later with the image of the actor Paul Brody pitching forward on the stage, his blood seeping through his fingers, just as the script had called for.

But this was real life. He'd been stabbed to death by someone I might well have spoken with that evening, or might spend time with the following day. Despite my efforts, sleep returned only in fitful spurts of a few minutes at a time, and I finally gave up at five in the morning, groggy and out of sorts but even more determined to get to the bottom of things.

Chapter Thirteen

In what book did Dame Agatha Christie introduce her enduring character Miss Marple?

I looked out the window of my room and noted that the snow had begun to abate, although it was still falling, the flakes larger and fatter than they'd been during the night. According to veteran weather watchers back home in Cabot Cove, a change from small to large flakes meant we were on the trailing edge of the front, with clearing on the horizon. Their predictions were usually accurate—no surprise considering how many of them made their living out in the elements and depended upon their observations and experience.

But even though it was snowing less hard, the damage had been done. The narrow, corkscrew road leading up the mountain to Mohawk House looked impassable. Hopefully, heavy equipment from the town would soon be pressed into service to augment machinery owned by the hotel. In the meantime, anyone with a notion to leave had better own a good pair of snowshoes or cross-country skis and possess a healthy constitution.

It was too early for breakfast to be served in the dining room, and the brochure of hotel services in my room indicated that room service wouldn't be available for another hour. I changed into a light-weight sweat suit I usually travel with and did a half hour of stretching exercises, finishing up with running in place to get the blood flowing. By the time I'd showered and dressed for the day in a plaid wool skirt, burgundy blouse, and wheat-colored cardigan sweater, it was almost time for the dining room to open.

I went to the door, drew a deep breath—*What does this day have in store?*—opened it, and headed for breakfast.

I noticed on my way to the dining room that the same officers were posted at various exits who'd been stationed at them during the night. Thanks to the snow, there wasn't any chance of their being relieved. I hoped Detective Ladd would come up with a scheme to allow for some sleep time.

As I entered the dining room, it appeared that I was among very few guests there at that hour. But as the hostess led me to the authors' table, I realized that there were more people than I'd initially seen. Detective Ladd sat alone at a small table partially hidden by a column and potted ferns. He glanced up and nodded as I passed, and I returned his nod. Once seated, I looked to the opposite side of the room and saw the flamboyant redheaded woman who'd engaged in the argument with a couple during check-in and who'd almost bowled me over in the hall.

Two tables away from her was the couple in matching sweaters. They'd exchanged the argyle cardigan and vest for a pair of heavy wool pullovers with a Scandinavian pattern in blue, gray, and red. They wrapped some food in a napkin and left the dining room.

Jody, our waitress from dinner, looked exhausted as she came to the table to see whether I wanted coffee and juice.

"Working dinner *and* breakfast, I see," I said.

"No choice," she replied, "not with the storm. My replacement couldn't get here this morning, so I'm on double duty, like everybody else."

"Well," I said, hoping to boost her flagging spirits, "I'm sure the plows will get here soon and things will get back to normal."

"I sure hope so," she said. She looked around to see that we weren't being overheard, then leaned closer and asked, "Is Mr. Chasseur really a Hollywood producer?"

"He's ah—he has spent time in Hollywood, and he and his wife"—I stressed the word "wife"—"live there. Why do you ask?"

"He told me that I was perfect for a movie he's producing and wants me to read for him."

"Here?"

"In his room later today."

"I see." I, too, ensured that no one else was listening before I added, "Maybe it isn't a good idea to go to his room to audition, Jody. My suggestion is that you ask him to give you the script to read at your leisure, and tell him that you'll be happy to audition for him at a later date, perhaps in California."

She snorted softly. "Like I'll ever get to California."

"If you do decide to read for him today, insist it be in one of the public rooms, or at least that his wife be present. Do things the proper way."

"I thought that, too," she said. "Frankly, he's creepy, like a dirty old man."

I pursed my lips, resisting a smile. "I wouldn't know about that, Jody, but I think you're a very smart girl. What would you recommend for breakfast?"

"The breakfast buffet for sure, Mrs. Fletcher. Can I get you anything right now?"

"A cup of tea and an orange juice would be nice, thanks."

By now, a number of people had arrived, and the huge dining room's deathly silence had been broken by their conversations. Several guests greeted me as I perused the table of hot breakfast items, settling on a freshly made omelet from a chef in whites who deftly flipped it and slid it onto my plate. A few strips of bacon and a bowl of fruit completed my selections, and I carried them to the table where Georgie Wick and her friend, Harold Boynton, he of the wandering hands, were now seated.

"Good morning," I said.

"Good morning," they responded.

"Sleep well?" Boynton asked.

"Not especially," I said, "but I doubt whether anyone did last night."

"I slept like a rock," he said, chuckling. "Dead bodies don't bother me. Spent my entire adult life in the morgue frolicking with them. They make surprisingly pleasant companions. Never argue with you." He laughed heartily and excused himself to go to the buffet.

"How about you?" I asked Georgie. "Sleep all right?"

"Barely a wink," she said as she limply sat back in her chair.

"I understand," I said as I started on my breakfast.

"I'm almost afraid to mention it," she said.

"Mention what?" I asked

"What I saw after leaving you last night."

I placed my fork on the plate, dabbed at my mouth with my napkin, sat back, and allowed my quizzical expression to ask the obvious question.

"I saw him."

"Him?" Was she about to tell me that her former lover, the young man who'd died, had paid her a nocturnal visit? Mohawk House did have a history of ghost sightings, if you believed the stories, and Ms. Wick had a history of seeing ghosts.

"The actor." She said it so softly I wasn't sure I heard her correctly.

"Actor?" I asked. "Which actor?"

"Paul. The one who was shot."

"You saw Paul?"

She nodded.

"I thought the medical examiner removed his body."

"He looked so alive to me."

"I'm certain you must be mistaken."

As Boynton headed back to the table, she placed her index finger against her lips. I got the message and concentrated on my food. But my mind couldn't focus on an omelet or bacon. What was she talking about? Had she conjured a vision of the slain actor? She'd said Paul reminded her of her lover. Had she dreamt of her former sweetheart and replaced the image of his face with one of Paul's? Or had the ME not been able to negotiate the mountain in the storm and returned with the body? Georgie could have stumbled upon where the ME and Detective Ladd had taken the corpse. If so, I'd like to see it again myself. Obviously, I wouldn't get any answers as long as her corpulent friend was around.

Chasseur joined us. He wore a T-shirt and the same sandals as the previous evening, black socks his only concession to the weather outside. He rubbed his hands together, grinned, and looked around. "Lovely morning."

"Your wife's sleeping in?" I asked.

"Not feeling well," he said, the grin never wavering. "She gets these bouts of psychosomatic illness once in a while."

A fist to the eye isn't psychosomatic, I thought.

Jody came to the table, and Chasseur turned his full attention to her, his eyes moving up and down the ample, youthful body that was evident despite her uniform.

"Would you like coffee and juice?" she asked.

He leered. "I won't tell you what I really want," he said. "Maybe when we get to know each other a little better."

"Jody says you're interested in her for a part in a film," I said.

He glared at me, then looked up at Jody and said, "It was supposed to be our little secret."

She looked at me, smiled, and walked away without getting his order.

"Cute kid, huh?" he said, going to the buffet.

"Quite a fellow," Boynton said between bites from a plate laden with sausage, bacon, and waffles swimming in syrup. "Tells me all of his books are being made into films. Are your books in the cinema, too, Jessica?"

"A few have been made into movies, but certainly not all of them."

Boynton poked Georgie with his elbow. "Better get yourself a new agent, Georgie, eh? Yours doesn't seem to be doing his job."

"My books are difficult to translate into film," Georgie said, straightening in her chair. "Ah don't like the way Hollywood treats the black arts, and ah'd rather control the images my readers see than let some young film school grad make my books look like a warmed-over combination of Halloween and Mardi Gras."

"Still, you could make a bundle," he said, popping

the last of his waffle into his mouth. "Might be worth the sacrifice."

"Were you happy with the results, Jessica?" Georgie asked.

"With the film versions of my books?"

She nodded.

"The first one was an interesting experience," I said. "I'll grant you that. But the final product was so different from what I'd written that I think they just wanted to use my title, but not my plot. During the shoot, I tried to convince the producer to change it back, but they had a budget and a schedule to keep, so my advice went unheeded. It did well at the box office, but I can't say I felt it was truly mine."

"And the others?"

"After the initial encounter with the way Hollywood works, I decided it was probably wise not to watch the process again. Much better for the digestion." I took a sip of tea and smiled at her.

"You make my point," she said primly. "Ah couldn't stomach it if they changed my vision of the characters I spent so much time developing."

Harold patted his stomach and burped behind a fist. "Splendid food," he said, sighing, then placed both hands on the edge of the table and pushed his chair back. "I think I'll see what I missed the first time round. If you ladies will excuse me."

"So," I said as soon as Harold had ambled out of earshot, "tell me more about what you saw last night."

"Ah know y'all will think it strange," she said, her

Southern accent deepening, "but it's true. Couldn't sleep and took a walk around the hotel. Sometimes ah do that at night, wander about. It's when some of the best ideas for my novels come to me."

"I hope you carry a pad and pen with you," I said lightly.

"Oh, yes, always do. Anyway, ah was walking in a hallway on the top floor—it must have been three or four o'clock this morning—when he just appeared."

"Paul, the actor who was killed."

"Yes. It was only a fleeting glance, no more than a second or two. He was coming out of a room. I think he saw me, because he quickly vanished back inside."

"You're quite sure it was Paul? Couldn't it have been someone else?"

"Oh, no. I have very sharp vision. He put his hand to his chest, right where the wound had been—I saw the blood—and floated—that's what it looked like—back into the room."

"That's, um—that's really interesting, Georgie," I said, fumbling for what to say. I felt like the people who attend a terrible theatrical production in which a friend is appearing, and who must come up with a comment when they go backstage after the curtain has fallen. *"Very interesting."* Noncommittal. No harm done, no feelings hurt.

"You probably don't believe me," she said softly as Chasseur returned from the buffet line.

"So," he said, once seated, "what's the latest on the murder?"

I shrugged. So did Georgie.

"Why do I have the feeling that you two are cooking up something, hatching a plot?" he said. He didn't give us time to reply before he looked around the dining room for Jody, spotted her, and waved her to the table. "Where's my coffee and juice?" he asked.

"You didn't order it," she said.

"Well, I am now. You want to be in the movies, you'd better get on the ball, sweetheart."

She walked away, and I said, "She's right. You didn't order it when she asked earlier. You were too busy—"

"Too busy *what*?"

"Nothing," I said. "The next act of the play is in an hour, and we have the authors' panel later today. I'll see you there."

"I'll go with you," Georgie said. "I don't want anything to eat."

We left Chasseur sitting alone and exited the dining room. Boynton had taken his second overflowing plate and joined the redheaded woman who'd been eating alone. He must have said something amusing to her because she laughed loudly, her fingertips pressed to her lips as though whatever he'd said was naughty.

The hallway was warm, the radiators along its length hissing. "My, it feels like summah in New Orleans," Georgie said, tugging on her collar.

"It must be difficult to keep the temperature even in an old building like this," I said.

"He's a very difficult man, isn't he?" she said as we ambled toward the main lobby.

"John Chasseur?"

"Yes. He makes me uncomfortable."

"Why?"

"I have the feeling there's something evil in his spirit, but he can't help it. Perhaps he's struggling against the demons, just not successfully yet."

"You're being kind," I said, thinking if Chasseur had demons, he was more likely to embrace them than fight them off.

"Ah always try to be kind, Jessica. Sometimes it hurts me."

"There isn't enough kindness in the world," I said, mentally chastising myself for expressing my negative thoughts aloud. We rounded a corner and approached a room in which a dozen or so weekend guests were gathered. The man who dressed in concert with his wife spotted us as we passed, came from the room, and said, "Excuse me, Mrs. Fletcher, Ms. Wick. I've been hoping to talk to you this morning. My name's Sydney Pomerantz."

Mr. Pomerantz was a beefy man of medium height. His complexion was sallow, almost gray, his eyes cobalt blue and sunk deeply into their sockets. Sparse strands of white hair went off in a dozen different directions. He'd taken off his Scandinavian sweater, and wore a blue button-down shirt. A card with the room key attached was tucked into the breast pocket, the number 3 just visible.

"Pleased to meet you," I said, taking his hand. Georgie Wick shook it, too.

"I hope I'm not imposing on your morning," he said.

"Not at all," I said.

"I don't know whether this is breaking the rules," he said, "but Mrs. P. and I have a question about something in the play. I thought you might be good enough to help." He had a speech tic that resulted in a guttural sound coming from his throat every dozen words or so, sort of a "glug." Probably a nervous habit rather than something physiological, I thought.

I looked at Georgie, whose expression said she didn't know anything about rules.

"What's your question?" I asked.

"You see," he said, "I noticed during the scene that happened outside the dining room last night, the one with the actor Paul threatening the older gentleman, that Paul hid the gun on his person. Now that he's been shot"—he coughed to cover his vocal tic—"my wife and I wondered whether it could have been a self-inflicted wound, or even an accident. Would we be too far off the mark to include that in our deliberations with the other team members?" He smiled sheepishly. "I wouldn't want to look foolish in front of them, you know."

"Mr. Pomerantz," I said, "I don't know anything

about the rules, but all I can say is that in productions put on by the Savoys, anything is possible. Anything! Rule nothing out. I assure you there will be many people who will be far off the mark by the time the weekend is over. No one will look foolish, but everyone will have had lots of fun."

His wife, who'd also doffed her sweater and wore a blue shirt, came from the room and said, "Now, Sydney, don't you be bothering the writers. I'm sure they have better things to do than talk with you."

"Oh, no," I said, "it's a pleasure to—"

His wife wasn't listening. She grabbed his arm and led him back into the room, where their team members were deep in conversation, a trail of apologies from him echoing behind them.

Georgie and I continued down the hall and went into a room just off the auditorium where the play would be performed in an hour or so. We took chairs by a window. "Now," I said, "tell me more about this sighting of yours last night."

"There's really nothing more to tell, Jessica. I saw him come from a room and step into the hallway. It was dark, shadowy. He saw me coming and disappeared back inside."

"How could you be sure it was Paul if it was so dark?"

A small pout inhabited her mouth. "It wasn't that dark," she said defensively.

"Do you think this was an apparition?" I asked.

"His spirit, you mean," she said, brightening. "Of course. It must have been. I'm very sensitive to them, you know. They make themselves visible to me. Sometimes, when they materialize, they look so substantial, they fool us into thinking they're alive." She looked at me. "They do," she insisted.

"I'm not doubting you," I said.

"Yes, you are," she said.

She was right, of course. Paul Brody had been murdered. We all stood over his body. Whether he died of a gunshot wound or a stabbing made little difference, at least from the standpoint of GSB Wick's tale. The man was dead. The only conclusion I could come to as we sat there, the snow falling behind us outside the window, was that she had a very active imagination, and perhaps more of a problem with alcohol than I'd realized. One thing was certain: GSB Wick, bestselling author of murder mysteries involving the supernatural, was—different.

After I assured her a few more times that I hadn't doubted her story and was just trying to get the facts straight, she excused herself, saying she wasn't feeling well, and left me alone. I heard noise from the auditorium and was about to see what was going on when Detective Ladd walked in.

"Good morning, Mrs. Fletcher. Enjoy breakfast?"

"Yes, thank you. You?"

"I suppose so. What I need is some sleep rather than food, but you need fuel to keep the ol' engine running."

"That's important," I agreed.

"A question."

"Yes?"

"After breakfast I saw you talking to an older man in the hall."

"Yes. He's part of the murder mystery group. His name is Pomerantz, I believe. Sydney Pomerantz."

"Not his real name."

My eyebrows arched. "Oh? How do you know that?"

"He's a local. He's been in the papers."

"Is he a politician or a businessman?"

"He's an accused murderer."

"Accused, you say. Not convicted?"

"Right. Seems Mr. Sydney Pomerantz—his real name is Sydney Powell—came home from work early one summer day ten years ago—he was in construction, actually worked on one of the wings that was added here at Mohawk House—and found his wife strangled to death on the kitchen floor."

"How horrible. You say *he* was accused of having done it?"

"Right again. The local DA tried to build a case against him but didn't have enough evidence to go on, so it was dropped."

"They never accused anyone else of killing her?"

"Nope. It's a cold case. But every once in a while I pull out the file and go over it. Looks bad for the department to have an unsolved murder."

"He's obviously remarried," I said. "His wife is here with him."

"Yeah, I know. They got married a month after his wife was killed, which makes people even more suspicious."

"I can imagine it would."

"Funny thing about it, though," Ladd said.

"Can murder ever be funny?" I said.

"No, but sometimes strange things come out of it. You notice how he talks?"

"You mean that sound from his throat."

"Yup. The way people in town figure it, that sound is his punishment for what he did to his wife. God works in strange ways."

"So I've been told. You think he murdered his first wife so he could marry the second one?"

"That's one theory, but there was a young guy involved, too."

"Who would that be?"

"Don't know. Some laborer who came around the house to clean the pool, trim hedges, stuff like that. The scuttlebutt at the time was that the wife must've been having an affair with the laborer, and Pomerantz interrupted them in flagrante delicto, if you get my meaning, and killed her."

"But might it not have been the young man who killed Mr. Powell's wife?"

"So Pomerantz claimed. Said she was dead when he got home. Problem was, this laborer disappeared right after her body was found. Gone. Poof! Never heard from him again."

"No one knew his name?"

"Not that anyone admitted to. My former boss handled it, his last investigation before he retired and headed for Florida."

Ladd stood. "I'd better get going. I'm trying to

streamline the questioning of all the guests." He turned and looked out the window. "Still coming down."

He left. I got up, took my own look at the white stuff still falling from the heavens, and silently agreed with his assessment.

In the auditorium next door, I recognized Larry and Melinda Savoy's voices but couldn't make out what they were saying. I stepped through the doorway, about to greet them, when I heard Larry curse. He jumped up out of the chair in which he'd been sitting, knocking it over. It fell to the floor with a loud clatter.

"You don't know what you're talking about, Larry," Melinda said angrily, slamming something down on the table "You're just dredging up the past for no reason. That's ancient history. Do you hear me?"

"Yes, I do, and I have a long memory. Don't you forget it."

I cleared my throat to give away my presence. Larry's face lit up. "Good morning, Jessica," he said, too heartily.

Melinda turned, waved, and hurried backstage.

"How are you feeling?" Larry said, walking up the aisle to where I stood.

"A bit tired. Otherwise, fine. You?"

"The same."

"I hope I didn't interrupt anything serious."

"Serious? My wife is an actress and a playwright. Being a drama queen comes naturally to her. She's not happy unless she's emoting about something."

I'd never noticed that about Melinda, but decided not to challenge him.

He pulled me away from the door and lowered his voice. "Remember when you asked me whether I knew anyone in the cast or crew who might have had it in for Paul?"

"Yes, of course I do."

He looked around as the audience began filing into the room for the next performance. "Well, I might have an answer for you."

Chapter Fourteen

**What writer wrote nine books that featured
sustaining characters Grave Digger Jones and
Coffin Ed Johnson?**

I knew I couldn't press Larry at that moment, not
with the next act about to start. But I would try to
catch him as soon as it was over. Did he have some
solid information about a cast member that might
shed light on Paul Brody's killer? It certainly sounded
that way.

My thoughts shifted to Georgie Wick's bizarre
claim that she'd seen the deceased coming from a
room in the dead of night, and I was annoyed at
myself for neglecting to ask her the room's number.
I went to a house phone, and asked the operator to
connect me to Ms. Wick's extension. Harold Boynton answered.

"Hello," I said. "It's Jessica Fletcher."

"Of course it is," he said in his British baritone.
Like many Englishmen I've known over the years,
he tended to laugh a lot as he spoke, swallowing
some of his words and making it difficult to understand him. We share the same English language,
but . . .

"Is Georgie there?"

"That she is, but she's in the loo. Glad you rang. I was telling her just this morning that you and I probably have a lot to talk about, lots in common. Up for a spot of tea?"

"Thank you," I said, "but it's a busy morning. Georgie said she wasn't feeling well and was going to her room."

"Upset stomach, that's all. She'll be tip-top in no time. Shame you're too busy. Would love to find some time alone with you. Lunch? Maybe we can sneak away from the others and—"

"I'll try and connect with Georgie later," I said, interrupting him. "Please tell her I called."

The seats in the auditorium were filling up. I looked around for an empty chair. I spotted John Chasseur sitting between two women, and deliberately made my way to the opposite side of the theater, where Detective Ladd stood leaning against a wall, his eyes taking in everyone as they entered and found seats. The various teams to which guests had been assigned, and those made up of friends who'd arrived together, staked out areas of the auditorium from which they could get a clear view of what was about to happen onstage. Ladd didn't acknowledge me as I casually sidled up to him—his attention was fixed on Sydney Pomerantz, aka Sydney Powell, and his wife, who'd taken seats with their fellow team members.

"What did he say to you earlier?" Ladd asked without turning to me.

"Mr. Pomerantz? He asked about what he considered a clue, and wondered whether he was breaking the rules by speaking about it with me."

A small smile crossed Ladd's lips. "*He's* worried about breaking the rules?" he said, his voice filled with irony. "Killing your wife is breaking the rules in my book."

"You said he was never tried for the murder," I said.

"Doesn't mean he didn't do it," he said, mimicking the throaty catch in Pomerantz's voice.

"Or that he did," I said. "Frankly, I can't conceive why someone accused of having murdered his wife would opt to attend a murder mystery weekend—in his hometown to boot."

"The way I hear it, he gave up his construction business shortly after his wife's death and has been devoting his life to finding her killer." He guffawed. "Sounds a bit like Mr. O. J. Simpson, doesn't it? At any rate, he and his new wife attend forensic conferences around the country trying to learn new techniques of solving crimes. Looks like murder mystery weekends like this one are on their agenda, too."

"Still," I said, "I can't imagine coming to one in my hometown. What do other people say about him?"

"He's a bit of a joke in town," Ladd replied, "with that catch in his throat and speculation about how and why it developed. I suppose he's used to it by now, lets it roll off his back. I agree with you. If I was accused of something like that, I'd leave town pronto and get as far away as possible. Maybe that'll be his undoing, hanging around."

"You sound as though you're still trying to build a case against him."

"Officially, it's a dead case, but I keep it open, at least in my mind. One of these days . . ."

The theme from *The Pink Panther* suddenly came from large speakers suspended at the front of the auditorium, causing an almost visceral change in the guests' mood. The Savoys liked to begin their presentations with music befitting the event. Toes tapped, and some hummed along with the familiar melody. A few minutes later, everyone turned to see Larry Savoy march down the center aisle to the stage. The music stopped, a hush fell over the audience, and Larry picked up his wireless, handheld microphone.

"Everyone have a good night's sleep?" he asked, mischief in his voice.

A flurry of answers came from the audience. A man stood, waited for the chatter around him to end, and said loudly, "I've been to other shows you've put on, Mr. Savoy, but I've never seen one like this. We not only have to figure out who murdered the young guy, Paul, onstage, but we're told he might really have been killed. Is that true?"

Larry smiled and held up his hand against a supportive chorus for what the man had said. "Why don't you just sit back and enjoy the experience?" Larry suggested.

"Was the young actor murdered?" a woman asked. "I mean, not a phony murder but a real one."

Larry started to respond, but another man jumped to his feet. "My wife and I were questioned by that detective over there," he said, pointing at Ladd. "I think he's a real cop, not an actor."

One of the women who'd approached Detective Ladd and me in the bar the previous night piped up next. "I think he is part of the play, but he won't talk to us. I thought all the actors were supposed to answer our questions. It's not fair."

"Please, please," Larry said, "let's all calm down. You'll find plenty of answers to your questions in the second act. And don't forget, a member of the team that comes up with the best answer, and puts on the best skit, wins a free weekend here at the magnificent Mohawk House." He ignored further comments from the audience and read the next set of questions that had been supplied by me and the other writers, with additional ones from the Savoys. A few minutes later, he instructed Melinda to collect the cards. Once she had, Larry announced, "All right now, the second act is about to begin. Pay attention. Use every ounce of deductive power you possess, and make sure the person next to you doesn't have blood on his or her hands." He ended with a wicked chuckle and returned to the rear of the auditorium.

The lights dimmed and the audience became silent. The curtain opened slowly to reveal the same set as had been used in the opening act. On the stage were Cynthia Whittaker, her father, Monroe, and the two police officers, Detective Nick Carboroni and Officer Clarence Dolt. Carboroni held center stage. He wore his trench coat à la the TV detective Columbo, and his fedora was at an extreme angle, almost completely covering one eye. Officer Dolt stood a few paces behind him, arms crossed, a know-it-all expression on his face.

"All right," Carboroni said as he paced the stage, "lemme get this straight. You say the desists—"

Dolt tapped his boss on the shoulder. "It's deceased, Boss," he said. "Not desists."

"I know, I know," Carboroni snapped. "And I told you a hundred times never to correct me when I'm in the midst of interrograting suspects."

"You mean interrogating," Dolt said.

Monroe Whittaker stepped between the two cops. He snarled at Carboroni, "Do you mean to tell me that I'm being considered a suspect?"

"Yes sir. The way I figure it, everybody who was here is a suspect. Right outta the manual."

"This is absurd," Monroe said, waving away the notion that he might be under suspicion.

"I'm told you and the deceased didn't get along too good," the stage detective said. "That true?"

"If you mean I didn't like the young man, you're absolutely right. He had designs on my daughter despite being her inferior in class, style, and everything else that matters."

Carboroni turned to where Cynthia sat on the couch, her fist pressed against her mouth. "I hate to bother you at a time like this," he said, "but I've got a dead body on my hands. You and the deceased had something going between you?"

She removed her hand from her mouth and said, "We were going to be married."

"Over my dead body," said her father.

"Only the dead body wasn't yours," Carboroni said to Monroe. To Cynthia: "You ever hear your father threaten your finance?"

"My *what*?"

"Finance. The guy you were going to marry."

"You mean fiancé," Monroe said disgustedly.

"Yeah, whatever. Well, young lady?"

"My father hated Paul," she replied. "It was no secret."

"What've you got to say about that, Mr. Whittaker?" the detective asked.

"I may have disliked the boy, but not enough to commit murder."

The actors turned as Victoria Whittaker entered the room. She was dressed in high style, more befitting attendance at a big-ticket society event than a murder investigation. She carried an oversized handbag, which she placed on a coffee table.

"Just the person I wanted to see," Carboroni said.

"I'm afraid I only have a moment," Victoria said, checking her appearance in a mirror. "I'm due at a luncheon."

"Yeah, well, maybe you'll have to change your plans," Carboroni said. "I've got a dead body here and—"

Victoria sighed loudly enough to be heard at the rear of the theater. She gave her hair a final touch with her fingertips, went over to her handbag, opened it, and pulled out a revolver.

"Hey, lady, put that down," Carboroni said.

"Yeah, lady, put that down," Dolt echoed, eliciting a scowl from Carboroni.

"Here," Victoria said, thrusting the weapon at Carboroni, who reacted by jumping back. "I assumed you might be looking for this." She handed the gun to the detective and turned to her husband. "I'm terribly sorry, Monroe, dearest, but as the detective says, we do, after all, have a dead body to deal with."

"Who owns this?" Carboroni asked.

"I, ah—I think it might be mine," Monroe said.

"That so?" the detective said, turning the weapon over in his hands as though it might provide a visual clue. "You *think* it might be yours. *Think?*" He placed the end of the barrel to his nose and inhaled with gusto, causing some audience members to laugh. Carboroni turned to them and said, "This is no laughing matter." He told Monroe, "This here weapon smells like it's been fired recently."

"If so," Monroe said, "it wasn't fired by me."

Monroe now faced his wife, who was poised to leave for her luncheon. "Have you gone mad?" he demanded.

"Oh, darling," she said, kissing his cheek, "don't be angry with me. When Catarina showed me where you'd hidden this vile thing, I felt I hadn't a choice but to do my civic duty and turn it over to the authorities."

"Who's Catarina?" Carboroni asked.

"Yeah, who is this Catarina?" Dolt asked.

"Shut up!" Carboroni growled.

"Catarina is our maid," Victoria said. "She isn't an especially thorough cleaner, but she's pleasant enough—and, I might add, honest. Toodle-loo." She flounced from the stage, bringing forth a smattering of applause. Cynthia ran after her.

Monroe started to leave the stage, too.

"You stay right here," Carboroni ordered. He told Dolt to keep an eye on Monroe.

"Where are you goin'?" Dolt asked.

"To find this Catarina lady." Carboroni said to the audience, "I got a feeling—just a hunch, but my hunches almost always are right—I got this hunch that this maid who don't clean so good might have something v-e-r-y interesting to tell us."

"I knew the maid had something to do with this," a man in the audience said loudly to a team member as Carboroni left Dolt and Monroe onstage.

As the act continued, I observed the audience, who were paying rapt attention to the onstage business. The line between a theatrical production about murder and the actual thing had become remarkably blurred that weekend at Mohawk House. I didn't know whether that was good or bad, only that while the farcical investigation was taking place among the actors and actresses, a very real investigation was under way.

I'd become so engrossed in the production, I hadn't noticed that Detective Ladd had left my side and now stood at the rear of the auditorium, where he was engaged in what appeared to be a whispered conversation with Georgie Wick. She'd obviously enjoyed that miraculous cure her friend Harold Boynton had suggested. Was she confiding in Ladd about her supposed sighting of the fallen Paul Brody? If so, I thought, she was not likely to find a sympathetic ear. Ladd didn't strike me as the sort who would believe in resurrected bodies and ethereal spirits. Neither did I, although I was not rigid enough in my beliefs to summarily dismiss such things simply because I hadn't personally experienced them.

I decided to stay through the end of the second act. The silliness onstage was preferable to having to ponder true crime—a welcome diversion, if only for a few minutes. But as the actor playing Detective Carboroni had said to the audience, I, too, had a hunch—that pleasant diversions would be few and far between over the next couple of days. And like his, my hunches almost always prove to be true.

Chapter Fifteen

The daughter of a former U.S. president has written more than twenty murder mysteries set in Washington, D.C. Who is she?

The rest of the second act went smoothly. I've always been impressed with the way the actors and actresses chosen by the Savoys were able to ad-lib, both on-stage and with members of the audience. The scripts used in the productions, written by Melinda Savoy, were loosely constructed, leaving plenty of room for improvisation.

Carboroni returned to the stage with the maid, Catarina, in tow, and she histrionically overplayed the fear she was supposed to be experiencing at having to face her employer, the formidable Monroe Whittaker. It was all entertaining theater, and the audience enjoyed it immensely. The act ended with Catarina loudly denying that she'd found Monroe's weapon and given it to his wife. There was more comic interplay between Carboroni and Dolt, broad, slapstick humor that had the onlookers laughing heartily. Of course, a Savoy production would not be complete without the actor who played the detective coming into the audience and questioning those who looked

as though they might provide interesting, funny answers. The curtain closed with Catarina standing center stage and pleading for someone to come forward
and help her. A couple of people started to do just
that, but Larry Savoy stepped in front of them and
announced, "Before you commit yourself to helping
Catarina, think twice. She may not be the innocent
young woman you think she is." He started to put
down the mike, then raised it to his mouth again and
said, "Detective Carboroni and Officer Dolt will be
making a special effort to interrogate more of you
today. Be careful what you say—or *you* may end up
in a pair of cold steel handcuffs."

I slipped out of the auditorium the moment the
curtain closed. I could find Larry later. I wanted to
see where Georgie Wick and Detective Ladd had
gone. They weren't in the immediate vicinity, so I
headed down a hallway in the direction of the private room Mark Egmon had provided for the detective. The door was shut when I approached, but I
could hear Ladd's voice and that of a woman
through it. I looked around to ensure I was alone.
Satisfied, I pressed my ear to the door and strained
to hear what was being said. Ladd's voice was the
softer of the two; the woman's was more clearly
audible.

". . . And, yes, I fired off the pistol when the script
called for it," she said.

"Where?"

"Offstage, in the hallway that leads backstage."

"And you saw no one else in that vicinity?"

"No. I was alone and—"

"Ah, Jessica. Always with an ear to the ground—
or in this instance, to the door."

I turned to face John Chasseur. He was grinning,
his pearly white teeth vivid against his tanned face.

"Goodness! You startled me," I said.

"Eavesdropping, I see. Is that how you get information for your books?"

"On occasion," I said, embarrassed to be caught.

The door opened. Detective Ladd looked from me
to Chasseur, his quizzical expression asking the obvious question.

"I was just about to knock," I said.

Ladd ignored me and asked Chasseur, "Something
I can do for you?"

"As a matter of fact, there is," Chasseur said. "No,
to be more accurate, there's something I can do for
you."

I looked past Ladd and saw Laura Tehaar, the
young woman in charge of props and costumes for
the Savoys, standing by the window. I already knew
she was there, of course, by the snippets of conversation I'd heard through the door. She'd obviously
been crying. She looked at me with wide, wet eyes.

Ladd started back into the room, stopped, turned
and said, "Mrs. Fletcher, got a minute for me?"

"Of course."

"Ms. Tehaar was just leaving." Ladd said it loud
enough for her to hear. She walked past us, a tissue
pressed to her nose and mouth.

I followed Ladd into the room, Chasseur so close behind he was almost against me.

Ladd said, "Mr. Chasseur, maybe we can get together later today."

"I thought you were a detective," Chasseur said.

Ladd cocked his head and grimaced.

"I thought you'd benefit from some insight," Chasseur said. "I've been keeping my eyes and ears open, and believe me, there are plenty of likely suspects. That's one of the strengths of my novels. I develop suspects like nobody else in the business."

"Sure," said Ladd, "always happy to have input in a case. But right now I've got something to discuss with Mrs. Fletcher. Can you come back, say, in a half hour?"

"It might be possible," Chasseur said, annoyed at being put off.

He turned to leave, but Ladd stopped him with, "By the way, I do have a question for you, Mr. Chasseur."

"Do you? Maybe later."

"Maybe now," Ladd said. "Were you in the auditorium when the young man was killed?"

Chasseur screwed up his face in exaggerated thought. "Of course I was. Why?"

"I've been developing a list of people who were in the auditorium and those who might not have been." Ladd said. "Most people have someone else to vouch for them, people on their teams, folks sitting next to them, things like that. I know Mrs. Fletcher was there because people said she was. Hard to miss a celebrity like her."

His comment didn't sit well with Chasseur, who frowned and pressed his lips tightly together.

"Well?" Ladd said. "Anyone with you in the theater when it happened?"

A forced laugh came from Chasseur. "I love it," he said. "Making me a suspect. I'll call my publicist in Hollywood. We can make some media hay out of this."

"Yeah, you do that," Ladd said. "In the meantime, if you come up with somebody who saw you there, let me know. Thanks for stopping by. See you in a half hour."

Chasseur, still feigning amusement, left, and Ladd closed the door behind him. "Now, Mrs. Fletcher," he said, "what's with this friend of yours, Ms. Wick?"

"I'd hardly call her a friend, Detective. I just met her this weekend, although I have been a fan of her writing for quite some time. What are you getting at?" I remembered our previous conversation about GSB Wick when he'd indicated he found her a little strange.

"I had a talk with her this morning," he said.

"Yes, I saw you two together."

"She, ah—she told me something really weird."

I smiled. "I assume you mean having seen Paul Brody's ghost last night."

"You know about that?"

"Yes. She told me, too."

"And?"

"And what?"

"And what do you make of it?"

I laughed and shrugged my shoulders. "I think that she has a vivid imagination, Detective. That's one of the major strengths of her novels, her creativity. Plus, she sincerely believes in the supernatural."

"Maybe she saw that earl who got his head cut off here years ago. Know what I think?" he said.

"Tell me."

"I think she's a loony. Gives me the creeps with that black hair and pale face. Looks like a ghost herself."

"Oh, I think that's unnecessarily harsh," I said. "Frankly, I enjoy her way of looking at things. It's different, and I've always appreciated people who use their imaginations to entertain us with a different view of our world—provided, of course, that they aren't hurtful to others."

I didn't know whether or not he agreed with me because he didn't say anything.

"I tried to reach her this morning," I said, "to ask where exactly she thought she saw Mr. Brody."

"I asked her."

"What did she say?"

"She wasn't really sure, but said it was on the third floor at the rear of the building. I popped up there to take a look myself. There are three rooms in a corner, separated from all the others on that floor.

I figure they're suites or something. Could have been any one of the three." He gave me the room numbers.

"Well," I said, "I'm sure there's nothing to be concerned about. She thought she saw Paul, but it was probably someone else who reminded her of him."

"And that's just the thing."

"What's just the thing?"

"Ordinarily, I'd dismiss what she said as the ravings of a lunatic. Except—"

I waited.

"Except that she also told me she had this boyfriend back in New Orleans, an actor, who looked just like Brody."

"She mentioned him to me, too," I said. "Are you suggesting that she might have had a reason to shoot—to stab—Brody because of his resemblance to her former lover?"

"It crossed my mind," he said.

"I have to admit, it crossed mine, too," I said, "but I don't really think she did it. She seems too timid for murder. But of course, I could be wrong. Have you found the murder weapon yet?"

"Still working on it," he said. "Thanks for stopping by."

"My pleasure."

"Oh, and Mrs. Fletcher, I'd appreciate it if you didn't try to hear what's being said in this room."

"Detective, I hope you don't think that I would—" I stopped myself and laughed. "Guilty as charged," I said.

"Plea accepted. See you around. And watch your step when you go up to the third floor. There's a loose piece of carpet up in that corner."

Was my inborn sense of curiosity that evident? I wondered as I left the room and went to the elevators. He knew the first thing I would do after leaving him was to check out those rooms for myself. But as an elevator arrived, I ignored the opening doors and went to the desk, where the man I'd spoken with the night before was still on duty.

"Long shift," I said.

"Sure is," he said, "but they say the plows should be here this afternoon. All I want to do is get home and go to bed."

"I understand. May I ask you a question?"

"Yes, Mrs. Fletcher. How can I help you?"

"Someone told me there are three special suites on the third floor, back in a corner, at the rear of the building."

"That's right. We call them our VIP suites, only they really aren't that fancy, nothing like a presidential suite or anything. But they're bigger than other rooms."

"I'd love to see one," I said, "for when I come back to Mohawk House sometime in the future."

"I'd be happy to show them to you, Mrs. Fletcher, except they're occupied."

"I see," I said. I leaned on the desk, closing the distance between us. "Would you mind telling me which guests are in those suites at the moment? Perhaps if I asked them directly . . ."

The dilemma I'd posed was written all over his weathered face. "I really can't do that, Mrs. Fletcher," he said. "Hotel policy. Privacy."

"Of course," I said. "It's just that one of the reasons I'm here this weekend, aside from being on the author panel this afternoon, is to research the next novel I'm writing. Seeing the rooms would have been helpful, but of course I wouldn't ask you to breach hotel policy. Actually, the names of the people aren't important to me, just a sense of the sort of VIPs who reserve such suites."

He laughed. "Nobody real important," he said. "At least not that I know of. There's a couple in one of them."

"Oh, of course," I said. "Mr. and Mrs. Pomerantz."

"You know them?" he asked.

"Yes, I do," I said, amazed that my stab in the dark had been correct. "Any of the cast members in those suites?" I asked. "Mr. and Mrs. Savoy, the producers of the play?"

"No, ma'am. They're on the second floor. One of the better rooms, though."

"And they certainly deserve it."

"Miss Carlisle is there, too."

"Oh? I don't know her."

Now, it was his turn to become conspiratorial. He, too, leaned on the desk as he said, "A really strange lady, Mrs. Fletcher. Some of the guests have been complaining about her."

"Why?"

"Well, she's not very pleasant, they say. She's had a few run-ins with other guests."

A vision of the tall redheaded woman came to mind. "The woman with the red hair," I said.

He nodded and smiled.

"Actually," I said, "I think she's a member of the cast."

"That's right," he said.

"What I'm anxious to find out is what role she's playing," I said. "She hasn't been onstage yet."

"She told me she's not supposed to be on the stage, Mrs. Fletcher. She's one of Mr. and Mrs. Savoy's audience ringers. They've done their shows here before, and they always have a few people like her. Know what I think?"

"What?"

"I think that if I wrote the play, I'd have her killed."

"Interesting idea," I said. "Maybe she will be. Good talking to you. I'm glad to hear that the plows will be showing up soon. I hope you get some rest. As for me, it'll be nice to be able to go outside again and get some fresh air."

But fresh air was furthermost from my mind at that moment. Larry Savoy had something to tell me. Could it be that a cast member had a reason to kill Paul Brody? He certainly wasn't a popular member of the troupe. He'd been disrespectful, dismissive, and downright aggressive. Had he so alienated his fellow thespians that one of them took revenge backstage?

I'd become so engrossed with Georgie Wick and her supernatural sighting, and with Detective Ladd, that I'd almost forgotten what Larry had promised. I hurried down the hall toward the auditorium, where I hoped Larry could provide a better clue than the leads Melinda had written into her play. The other guests at Mohawk House weren't the only ones that weekend with a need to solve a murder.

Chapter Sixteen

Many actors have played Agatha Christie's famed detective, Hercule Poirot, in movies. Name three.

Larry was backstage giving the cast post-production notes when I arrived. I didn't want to interrupt, so I stayed in the wings and listened as he and Melinda ran down a list they'd compiled during the second act. It seemed to me that the points they made were minor, small adjustments for various members of the ensemble to incorporate into the next scene, which was scheduled for early that afternoon.

But when he came to Catarina, the maid, his tone changed. He had been upbeat and positive with the others. Now his voice hardened. "Damn it, Catarina," he said, "how many times do I have to tell you that you're not performing in an amphitheater? Sure, you're supposed to be upset, but you're not a wounded banshee. Tone it down before that grating voice of yours sends the whole audience running for cover."

I wasn't sure whether the actress was about to

erupt into tears or respond with an angry outburst. She did neither. She glared at Larry for what seemed an eternity before turning on her heel and stomping from the stage.

Larry shook his head and addressed the rest of the cast. "It went well. It looks like the decision to go ahead with the play is working. But we can't let up now. The audience will be all over you throughout the day, especially wanting to know whether Paul is really dead. Keep 'em guessing. Keep them here at the hotel. They say the plows will be getting to us this afternoon, which means those guests who want to leave will be able to. Mark Egmon from the hotel staff says that anyone cutting short their stay because of the murder will be eligible for a refund. Obviously, that's not good for Mohawk House's bottom line, so let's cooperate. I want us invited back again next year."

As the cast and crew dispersed, Larry joined me in the wings.

"What did you think?" he asked.

"You handled it very well," I said. "The audience certainly seemed to enjoy it."

"That's what counts," he said.

"Larry, you said you wanted to talk with me about a cast member who might have had reason to kill Paul."

"Right, but not here. Too many ears."

We went through a door at the rear of the wings and entered a narrow corridor that ran the width of the stage and led to a closet-sized space being used

as a wardrobe room. Once inside, he closed the door
and pushed aside a rolling clothes rack holding a
variety of costumes. "Here, sit," he said, making
room on a folding chair by dumping its contents—
props and wigs—to the floor. "Okay, Jessica, here's
what I wanted to tell you. According to Melinda's
script, Catarina, the maid, had an affair with Paul
back in New York. He jilted her and took up with
Cynthia. Anyway, when she learned that he was involved with this pretty, rich society type, she applied
for a job as a maid to the Whittakers so she could
be at their house to witness what was happening and
do what she could to throw a monkey wrench into
the romance. Melinda loves complicated plots."

"But wouldn't Paul the character have recognized
the maid?" I asked.

"Sure, except that she had extensive plastic surgery
in New York before coming up to the Whittaker
mansion."

I laughed. "It must have been *very* extensive surgery for him not to figure out who she is."

"I know, I know," Larry said, holding up his hand.
"Far-fetched, but you've seen our shows before. Everything is far-fetched. Like opera. If you insist on
reality in your entertainment, you won't like us or
opera. That's the fun of it. That's what brings out the
groans at the end when the audience is made aware
of all the unlikely things that go into solving the
crime. Some of them get annoyed, but they're in the
minority. At any rate, Jessica, that's how Melinda
wrote it."

"I see," I said. "But what does that have to do with Paul Brody's death?"

"It looks like Melinda's script isn't as fictitious as it seemed."

"Now wait a minute, Larry," I said. "You aren't telling me that Catarina underwent plastic surgery and—"

He shook his head. "No, no, not that part of it. I'm hearing from members of the cast who know Catarina and Paul that they really did have an affair back in New York. He jilted her, they say—dumped her pretty hard. When she heard he'd signed on with us to do a series of interactive murder mystery productions like this one, she auditioned, too. I understand he wasn't too happy that Melinda invited her to join the show, but of course we didn't know their history, and in any case he didn't have any say about it."

"He could have quit," I offered.

"And lose a steady paycheck? Do you know what a steady paycheck means to actors, Jessica? We pay union scale, which isn't a lot, but it's better than waiting tables." He smiled as he added, "Maybe you earn more being a waiter, but it ain't showbiz. Anyway, Paul was like thousands of other actors in New York, scraping by, running from one audition to another, taking acting lessons from this or that guru, and refusing to admit that their talent is marginal and that their acting days are numbered. It's especially true of guys like Paul. It was one thing when he was young and playing juvenile leads. He was probably pretty good at it, although the scuttlebutt is that his lousy attitude torpedoed his career in Hollywood."

"Victoria told me that Paul was older than he looked," I said.

"She's right."

I thought for a moment before saying, "If I'm hearing you correctly, you think Catarina had a motive to kill Paul because of the way he treated her back in New York."

"It's not out of the realm of possibility. I figure I should give you everything I know."

"Did you tell this to Detective Ladd?"

"No. I just heard about their relationship. I didn't know before."

"Do you think Catarina did it?"

"Murder him? I don't know. All I can tell you is that there have been times when I wanted to kill Paul Brody myself."

"His attitude?"

"That, and the trouble he was threatening to cause me with the union."

"Over what?"

"Rehearsals, not being paid overtime for ones that run a few minutes longer than the contract calls for."

"This may be a silly question, but why did you keep him in the cast? Surely there are plenty of other actors who could have played the role."

"I would have fired him in a minute," Larry replied, "but Melinda had a soft spot for him, claimed he added something special to the cast. I didn't see it and intended to get rid of him after this weekend. Looks like somebody else saved me the bother."

"Well," I said, "the scorned woman has always had a viable motive for murder. But there would have to be a lot more evidence before pointing a finger at Catarina. Most women who are jilted don't end up murdering their former lovers."

"You're right, of course. But don't the police always look first at those who had a motive to do a crime?"

"Yes, and a spouse or significant other, as they call it, is always highest on the suspect list."

There was a tap on the door. Jeremy, the stagehand, looked into the room. "Hey, Larry, we're moving some scenery back here," he said. "Don't open this door till we get it out of the hall, okay?"

"Sure, sure. Knock again when you're done."

"How long do you suppose they'll be?" I asked.

"Ten, fifteen minutes tops," Larry said, "unless it gets wedged in again. We had a time of it yesterday."

I didn't relish being cooped up with Larry in the wardrobe room if the scenery became unmanageable again. I looked past him to a pile of boxes and steamer trunks, behind which there appeared to be a door. "Where does that lead?" I asked.

Larry turned. "I have no idea," he said. "I never gave it any thought."

I got up, squeezed between the boxes and trunks, and tried to see through a dirty glass insert in the door's upper half. Embedded in the glass was a mesh screen of the chicken wire variety. I reached down behind the boxes, wrapped my hand around the doorknob, and turned. It opened easily.

"Do Detective Ladd and his officers know about this door?"

"Never occurred to me to tell them," he said.

"Help me move these things out of the way," I said as I pulled down the top box and handed it to him. A few minutes later the door was fully revealed. I pushed it open and stepped into a small room, no larger than ten feet square. Beyond it was a dark, narrow passageway. I squinted against the gloom and saw a spiral staircase at the far end.

"Coming?" I asked Larry.

"Where does it lead?" he asked.

"We're about to find out," I said as I started walking, slowly and deliberately, touching the wall with my hand in case I tripped over something. I stopped halfway to the staircase and turned to see if Larry was behind me. He remained standing in the open doorway, obviously ambivalent about proceeding.

I continued until I reached the foot of the stairs. Larry had now joined me. I started up, still taking cautious steps. The treads were extremely narrow, the risers taller than normal. My upward path came to an abrupt end at another door, this one leading to the outside. It, too, had glass with mesh embedded in it. I looked through it and saw only white—the snow continued to fall, adding to a large snowbank on a small terrace. The door had one of those horizontal bars you push to open. I glanced up and saw a sign: EMERGENCY EXIT-ALARMED.

"Nothing here," Larry said, a little out of breath from the climb.

I placed my hand on the bar.

"Better not open it," he said. "We'll have security coming down on us."

"The police should know about this exit to the outside," I said. "The killer might have escaped through it."

"Don't you think we would have heard the alarm, Jessica?"

I pushed on the bar. No bells or whistles sounded. I leaned against the door in an attempt to open it. It gave only a few inches because of the mound of snow on the other side.

"See anything?" Larry asked.

"Just snow," I said, pulling the door shut.

"Let's get out of here," he said. "It's eerie."

"If the killer escaped through this door," I said, "he or she would have left footprints in the snow. But any prints would have been well covered by now. Let's find Detective Ladd and tell him about this exit. It probably doesn't mean anything, but he should know."

As we turned to leave, two hotel security men appeared at the bottom of the stairs. "What are you doing up there?" one asked.

"We were just curious," I replied, leading Larry down to where they stood.

"That door's got a silent alarm," one of the uniformed men said. "You shouldn't have opened it."

"Sorry," I said. "We didn't mean to cause you any inconvenience."

"Yeah, well, don't go around opening emergency doors. There's a sign, you know."

"Yes, we saw it," I said. "By the way, who usually uses this door?"

"Nobody. It doesn't go anywhere."

"It looks like it opens onto a small terrace," I said. "I imagine it's lovely in good weather, overlooking the grounds."

One of the guards snickered. "That's where people say they see the earl," he said. "Other places, too, but guests claim they've seen him late at night out there, looking over his property. Did you see him?"

"With his head tucked underneath his arm," added the other.

"That's an old song," Larry said.

"Yes, it is," I said. "British." I asked the guards, "By any chance, did the silent alarm go off last night?"

"Doubt it," said a guard. "Engineering just fixed it this morning. Out of commission for a week."

"Sorry to have brought you up here on a wild-goose chase," I said. "We won't do it again."

The guards walked away, and we prepared to return to the wardrobe room. I took a final glance around and saw, for the first time, what appeared to be a trapdoor in the ceiling outside the door.

"Look at that," I said.

"Look at what?"

"It looks like my attic door at home. I wonder where *that* leads."

"Probably nowhere of interest, Jessica."

"Give me a boost," I said.

"Ah, come on," he said.

I looked around and spotted an empty plastic milk crate. I pulled it over beneath the trapdoor. "Give me your hand," I said, placing one foot on it. Larry obliged. With his hand to steady me, I climbed onto the crate and reached up, barely able to reach a short piece of rope attached to the door. I pulled. It was hinged on one end, and opened with a creaking sound. "Darn!" I said.

"What's the matter?"

"I can't get high enough to see what's up there."

"You can come back another time."

I grasped his hand again and stepped down from the crate. The trapdoor, which had some sort of spring attached to it, slammed shut, sending down a cloud of dust.

"Whew," I said, fluffing my hair to get the dirt out of it.

We returned to the dressing room, closed the door, and pushed the boxes and trunks against it again. Larry opened the door to the hall.

"Looks like they got the scenery through," he said. "Sorry to desert you, Jessica, but I have to run. I'm meeting with Egmon and his people."

"Thanks for coming with me," I said.

He gave me a funny smile. I followed him back to

the stage, came down into the auditorium, and we walked together to the main lobby. "Do you always have a need to explore dark places, Jessica?" he asked.

"Not always," I said, "but too frequently for some people, I'm sure. My friend Seth Hazlitt—he's a doctor back home in Cabot Cove—says I was born with an extra gene, a snoop gene."

Larry laughed and said, "I'd say your doctor friend has it right. See you at lunch."

I started to walk away, but he called my name.

"Yes?"

"The detective says that you'd bumped into Paul inside a doorway the first night you were here?"

"That's right."

"You said he was down there smoking a cigarette."

"Right again."

"That's funny. Paul said he'd quit."

"Lots of smokers find it difficult to stay off cigarettes. He probably didn't want you to know he'd started again."

"I would have given him a hard time, that's for sure. When he first got off cigs, he was a fanatic about it, drove some of the smokers in the cast and crew nuts with his preaching. Frankly, he was a pain in the neck on the subject."

"I didn't actually see him smoke, but when I opened the door, I saw him grind out a butt with his shoe."

Larry shook his head. "Doesn't surprise me that

Paul was a hypocrite about it. He was a hypocrite about a lot of things."

"Oh, Larry," I said, "you were going to give me a copy of the script."

"Right." He reached into a small briefcase with a shoulder strap that he seemed never to be without, pulled out a copy, and handed it to me.

"Thanks. Did you know that Paul Brody used to come here with his mother and father when he and his brother were kids?"

"No. Where did you hear that?"

"One of the staff told me. Anyway, thanks for the script. Forget about my saying that Paul was smoking when I first met him. I must have been mistaken."

But somehow I felt I hadn't made a mistake. I remembered coming in from the cold and being surprised that he was right there, and I could have sworn he had a cigarette in his hand.

Chapter Seventeen

Many writers of murder mysteries focus on a specific city or region. What places did (or do) the following writers regularly use as settings for their books? Lawrence Block, Raymond Chandler, Tony Hillerman, and Ralph McInerny.

Although my stomach was reminding me that lunch was now being served, I decided to go up to the third floor to check out the three VIP suites. Georgie claimed she'd seen the slain actor's ghost emerge from one of them during the night, which was highly unlikely but worth following up on. I now knew that Mr. and Mrs. Pomerantz occupied one of the suites, and that the flamboyant redheaded woman, whose last name was Carlisle, had another. Who was in the third?

I took the stairs rather than the elevator, a pretty good climb that got the blood flowing. I'm used to daily walks back home in Cabot Cove, and was feeling the lack of exercise. Inactivity makes my body, as well as my mind, feel sluggish.

The hallway leading past the guest rooms on the third floor was dimly lit, like the rest of the corridors in Mohawk House except those downstairs in the public areas. The boards beneath the carpeting creaked as I traversed them. They had shifted over the years, creating a roller-coaster effect that had caused the carpet's seams to pull apart in places. As I rounded a corner, I heard two women speaking in Spanish, obviously exchanging a funny story, judging from their laughter. They stopped the moment they saw me.

"Hello," I said. "*Buenos días.*"

"*Sí.* Hello, madam," one said.

"I think I might be lost," I said. "Is this where the special rooms for important people are?"

They looked at each other before one seemed to understand my question. "*Sí*, Señora," she said. "The big rooms, many rooms, two or three."

"Ah, yes, suites," I said. "I was looking for—I was looking for a friend of mine who has one of these rooms. Ms. Carlisle?"

They stared at me.

"She's, ah—she's very tall—*grande*—with *rojo* hair."

Now their laughter returned. One covered her mouth with her hand and looked away.

"Is she in this room?" I asked, pointing to one of three doors.

"No, no, madam. *Aquí.*" She pointed to another.

"Oh. And Mr. and Mrs. Pomerantz?"

"*Sí, Señor y Señora* Pomerantz." She indicated their door.

"Who is in this room?" I asked, pointing to the third door. "A young man?"

The one who seemed to speak the best English

shook her head. "No one is in there, madam. It is empty."

"I see. Well, thank you. *Gracias.*"

"*De nada.*"

I was about to leave when I noticed a fourth door in the area, much smaller than the doors on the guest suites, and without a number.

"What door is that?" I asked, pointing to it.

They shrugged.

I went to it and tried the knob. It was locked.

"Do you have a key for it?" I asked, indicating with my hand what I wanted.

"No, Señora."

I thanked them again and walked back toward the staircase. Obviously, Ms. Carlisle's reputation wasn't lost on the staff. The two maids evidently viewed her as a comic character. Hopefully, she was nicer to them than she seemed to be to the hotel's guests. But then I reminded myself that she was part of Larry and Melinda Savoy's entourage, according to the desk clerk. It was hard to imagine someone who wasn't playing a part being that overtly theatrical and obnoxious in real life. The question was, where and when would she contribute to the play's denouement?

It also crossed my mind as I made my way to the dining room that since she occupied one of the three suites on the third floor, she might be able to shed some light on what Georgie Wick claimed to have seen. Was there another young person in that part of the hotel who looked like Paul Brody? It wouldn't take much of a resemblance for another young man to be mistaken for the slain actor, not in the middle of the night in a poorly lighted hallway.

I looked for Ms. Carlisle as I progressed through the dining room to the table reserved for authors but didn't see her. Georgie Wick and Harold Boynton were already there when I arrived, each with an empty glass in front of them. Boynton got to his feet and extended his hand. I took it. He kissed my hand, which I could have done without.

I'd no sooner taken my chair when John Chasseur arrived and sat next to me.

"Your wife still not feeling well?" I asked.

"No, she's not. She's having room service." He spotted our waitress, Jody, and said in a loud voice, "Hey, sweetheart, where's my martini?" She made a face and quickly disappeared in the direction of the kitchen.

"So, Mrs. Fletcher, what has our resident super-sleuth come up with?" Chasseur asked.

"Not a thing," I said. "You seemed to be on to something this morning. Did you get a chance to tell Detective Ladd about it?"

"Yeah, but it was a waste of time. Talking to him is like talking to a rock. Trust me, with him doing the investigating, the murder will never get solved."

I ignored his comment and asked what it was that he'd shared with the detective.

He laughed and shook his index finger at me. "Not on your life," he said. "You're on your own, lady.

We'll see who puts the pieces together at the end of the weekend. In the meantime, let's eat, drink, and be merry." He looked again for Jody. "Dumb kid," he said.

Boynton, Georgie, and I listened to Chasseur's comments without reaction. Jody returned and took our orders, which included drinks for everyone but me.

"I see you've made friends with the tall redheaded lady," I said to Boynton.

He gave me a knowing grin. "Lovely lady, if I may say so," he said, "and interesting. Well traveled, extremely worldly. My kind of woman."

"Is she part of the cast?" I asked. "I heard that she is."

"Rather doubt it," said Boynton. "She's too refined to be in the theater."

Jody arrived with the others' drinks. Fortified with his martini, and evidently not satisfied with the current topic of conversation, Chasseur said, "Seen any ghosts lately, Georgie?"

She started to respond, but he interrupted her and turned to me. "Miss GSB Wick tells me she's been seeing ghostly images at night." To Georgie: "Right?"

"I don't appreciate your making fun of me," Georgie said, draining her drink.

"Ah, come on, Georgie, it isn't everybody who's capable of seeing dead men strolling the halls at midnight. What did he look like? Bloody? Big hole in his chest? Did he sing to you? Dance? Do a buck-and-wing?"

"Now see here, sir," Boynton said, pulling himself

up straighter in his chair. "You're insulting Ms. Wick, and I won't stand for it."

"It's all right, Harold," Georgie said.

"No, it is not all right," Boynton said. "Georgie has special powers of observation and insight that most people don't. If she says she saw the dead actor, she did!"

Good for you, Harold, I thought, seeing a decidedly good side of the corpulent, amorous, former medical examiner.

"Suit yourself, pal," Chasseur said as he signaled to Jody that he wanted a refill of his martini. While the days of the three-martini lunch were just a vague memory for most people, it obviously didn't apply to all.

"The snowplows are due here this afternoon," I said, changing the subject.

"Good," said Chasseur. "Why anybody would choose to live in a place like this is beyond me."

Boynton's defense of Georgie had left him red-faced and breathing laboriously. He finished what was on his plate, wiped his mouth, pushed back his chair, and belched loudly.

"You don't look too good, Pops," Chasseur said, smiling. "Past your bedtime?"

"You, sir, are a bloody bore," Boynton said.

Chasseur's laugh was nasty.

Boynton got up unsteadily, using the back of his chair for support. "I'm not feeling well," he said.

"Maybe you should lie down," Georgie said.

"Yeah, lie down, Pops," Chasseur said.

I watched the tiny Georgie help Boynton walk away from the table.

"That was cruel of you," I told Chasseur when we were alone.

"Just having some fun with the old coot. They're some pair, huh? He spent his life carving up dead bodies, and she sees people who've been shot dead walking around. Whew!"

Mark Egmon came up behind me and placed his hands on my shoulders. "All set for the panel this afternoon, Jessica?"

"I think so," I said.

"You, John?"

"As ready as I'll ever be," Chasseur said. "Frankly, I could do without it."

"Mark, can we catch up after lunch—say in fifteen minutes?" I said.

Egmon glanced at his watch. "Sure. I should be back in my office by then. Know where it is?"

"I do. I'll see you there."

After Egmon was gone, I said to Chasseur, "I understand you requested to be part of this weekend."

"Who told you that? Larry?"

"Yes." I paused. "I can't help but wonder why you're so unenthusiastic about being part of it if you wanted so much to participate."

"Larry doesn't know what he's talking about. And neither do you."

I should have been accustomed to his rudeness by now, but somehow I always expect people to behave well. My appetite had flown. I folded my napkin, placed it on the table next to my half-consumed meal, and rose. "I'll see you on the panel," I said and left.

I went to my room and took a closer look at the cigarette butts I'd picked up last night in the smokers' vestibule and from my balcony. The same brand had been smoked in each location. I thought back to what Larry Savoy had said about Paul Brody not smoking. Maybe Larry was right that Brody was hypocritical about his anti-smoking stance, sneaking a few puffs now and then when others couldn't witness it. But I considered it unlikely. From my experience, people who developed vehement opposition to something seldom strayed from that position. Besides, how long could he keep his secret from others? A theatrical cast and crew developed into a tight-knit group.

I was about to go downstairs to meet with Mark Egmon when the phone rang.

"Mrs. Fletcher?"

"Yes."

"My name is Todd Waisbren. I'm a reporter with the local paper."

Detective Ladd had cautioned me about this. Obviously, the murder at Mohawk House was no longer a secret.

"How can I help you?" I asked.

"Well, I've gotten word that someone was killed at Mohawk House, an actor in the theater group that's performing up there this weekend."

I said nothing.

"Is it true?" he asked.

"I'm really the wrong person to answer that question, Mr. Waisbren. I—"

"Detective Ladd is there," he declared.

Again, I neither confirmed nor denied.

"I know he's there, along with the whole town police force. Since you're a famous mystery writer, I thought I might get a comment from you about the murder."

"Frankly," I said, "my major concern right now is this incredible snowstorm we're experiencing. Are the plows on their way?"

"That's what I'm told. I'll be coming up right after they clear the road. Look, Mrs. Fletcher, I don't want to put you in an awkward position, but a murder at Mohawk House is big news. We haven't had a murder in the town since—well, since a woman was strangled ten or so years ago."

The Sydney Pomerantz case, I thought, only back then he was Sydney Powell.

"That may be," I said, "and I would like to be of help. I know how tough it is to develop information for a story. But I really have nothing to say."

"I understand," he said. "Fortunately, one of your colleagues wasn't so reticent."

"Oh?"

"I'm a big fan of John Chasseur and his Agent Benny series. When I heard he was going to be part of the weekend, I planned to come up and have him sign some books. But with the snow and all—anyway, he was good enough to fill me in on the murder. He's a really nice guy. I just wanted a few additional comments from another successful murder mystery writer, like you."

"I'm glad Mr. Chasseur was helpful to you," I said, "but I really must go. I'm late for an appointment."

"Sure. Maybe when I get there you'll feel freer to talk. Thanks for your time."

I wasn't at all surprised that Chasseur had been the one to grant an interview with the press. Had Detective Ladd given him the same admonition about keeping quiet? If so, he'd wasted his breath.

Mark Egmon was on the phone when I walked into his office. He gestured for me to take a chair, which I did while he continued his conversation. When he was through, he sighed and said, "The press knows about the murder. That was a reporter from the local paper."

"Mr. Waisbren," I said.

"How did you know?"

"I just got off the phone with him myself."

"Seems your buddy, Chasseur, spilled the beans."

"Yes, it does seem that way. Nothing can be done about it now. I suspect that when the plows clear the road, you'll have more than one reporter on the premises."

He rolled his eyes and groaned.

"Mark," I said, "I have a question for you."

"About what?"

"About your three VIP suites on the third floor."

"What about them?"

"Well I'm not sure how to put this. Ms. Wick was

up there late last night and claims she saw Paul Brody come out of one of those suites."

"The actor? He's dead."

I nodded.

"You know," he said, "Ms. Wick is a little strange."

"She is different," I said, thinking I'd have to come up with another description of Georgie before the end of the weekend.

"Is she all there?"

"I think she's a very smart woman. I don't know what her motive might be, but I suppose we can chalk up her claim to having a novelist's overactive imagination."

"If you say so."

"I prefer to explain it that way. It's my understanding that two of the three suites are occupied."

"Only two?"

"I think so. Of course, my sources might not know for certain. There's a Mr. and Mrs. Pomerantz in one, Ms. Carlisle in a second one."

"Carlisle? Oh, right, the big redheaded woman, part of Larry Savoy's cast."

"Yes. I'm surprised that a cast member was put up in a suite like that. I assumed they'd be in lesser rooms, probably doubled up."

"You're right. I can't think that we ran out of all the regular guest rooms. I'll check into it."

"Would you mind letting me know what you find out?"

"Sure. You're in a suite, too. A junior suite."

"Yes. It's lovely."

"There was a cast member in your suite before you came. Rooms were tight, so we did some juggling. As a matter of fact—I hope this won't upset you . . ."

I waited.

"Brody spent a night in your suite. He was doubled up, but I don't know who shared the room with him. We moved him to make room for you."

"That's interesting," I said. "Where was he moved to?"

"Don't know. I'll check that out, too."

"I'd appreciate it. How are the guests handling the news? Do they all know?"

"If the press knows, I've got to believe the staff does, and information gets around pretty quickly. I'd say the guests are handling it amazingly well," he said. "Half of them still aren't sure whether a real murder has taken place or not. The other half—if they believe it happened—seem to enjoy being involved. At any rate, no one has asked for their money back yet. Once the road is cleared, that might change. But for now, everything's pretty quiet."

"I'm glad to hear it. Thanks for your time." I checked my watch. "I'd better get going. The panel starts in fifteen minutes."

"I'll be there," he said.

"Oh," I said, "one other thing."

"Uh-huh?"

"There's a small door up in the area where the three VIP suites are located. Do you know where that leads?"

It was a warm laugh. "I haven't the foggiest idea," he said. "There are lots of strange doors in this old building. I've looked behind a few, with trepidation, I might add. Could be an old laundry chute or a dumbwaiter shaft. Some of them lead nowhere, nothing behind them except maybe storage. We keep them locked to discourage guests from wandering where they shouldn't."

"Do you have the keys to them?"

"I have the keys to everything," he said, smiling.

"Would you mind opening the one on the third floor for me after the panel?"

"Happy to. Mind if I ask why?"

"Just to satisfy my natural curiosity."

"That's good enough reason for me," he said.

Chapter Eighteen

*What writer created the Dortmunder gang in a
series of comic crime novels?*

The panel discussion was held in a room approximately half the size of the auditorium. It filled up quickly, and by the time Melinda Savoy, who moderated, asked for attention, most of the seats were occupied. While she prepared to introduce us, I leaned over to Georgie and whispered, "How is Harold feeling?"

"Not well," she said. "I'm worried about him."

"He should see a doctor."

"I told him that," she replied, "but he's stubborn. He says he doesn't need to see a doctor because he *is* a doctor."

I smiled and thought of Seth Hazlitt back in Cabot Cove, one of the most stubborn men I've ever known. But even Seth wouldn't hesitate to seek medical help if he needed it. Besides, since Boynton had spent his medical career dissecting dead bodies, I'm not sure he would be the best physician to diagnosis his own ailment—unless it was after the fact.

Melinda's introductions were lengthy and flowery.

Chasseur, who didn't seem to display any outward sign of his drink consumption at lunch, basked in the kind words Melinda used to describe his career. Georgie was next, and seemed uncomfortable at hearing all the praise Melinda heaped upon her.

I was last to be introduced. The minute she finished reading from the bio I'd provided, Chasseur said, "Everyone knows that Jessica Fletcher not only writes about murder, she has a reputation for solving real ones." He turned to me. "Making any headway, Jessica, with the r-e-a-l Mohawk House murder?"

I'd been looking out over the audience while Melinda read my bio, and noticed that Detective Ladd and two of his uniformed officers had taken seats along a wall to my right, far away from others. Ladd's wince summed up his reaction to Chasseur's comment.

"Jessica?" Melinda said when I didn't respond.

"Oh, sorry," I said. "I was thinking of something else. As to John's question, no, I'm as much in the dark as everyone else in the audience. I'm sure you and Larry will give us plenty of clues to help us solve the crime that's part of your production."

Had I successfully deflected his question and brought the audience back to the theatrical murder, rather than the one that had actually taken place? Judging from the expressions on the faces of the crowd, I knew the answer was a resounding no.

Melinda sensed my discomfort and quickly turned to Georgie, asking her about her work habits, and how her Southern roots, particularly New Orleans, contributed to her stories and books. She answered in that small, thin voice of hers, slowly, deliberately, her Southern accent deepening as she spoke. She went on for quite a while, and I thoroughly enjoyed hearing what she had to say. But some audience members grew restless, prompting Melinda to interrupt and ask me the same question, substituting New England for New Orleans.

When Melinda turned to Chasseur with a question, my stomach muscles tightened in anticipation of what he might say. But sitting through the answers Georgie and I had given seemed to have mellowed him; at least he didn't attempt to bring up the murder of Paul Brody again. Instead, he held forth on the link between book publishing and Hollywood, and told amusing anecdotes about his experiences with having a novel turned into a motion picture, including the fact that he'd met his beautiful wife on the set.

"Definitely one of the perks of moviemaking, if you've seen my wife," he said, setting off a wave of chuckling in the audience. He was altogether charming and entertaining, and I could see what might have drawn Claudette to him when they'd first met. Apparently he no longer practiced that charm on her. And I hadn't seen his wife recently, not since our encounter in the round room. I began to worry and made a mental note to go upstairs when the event concluded and knock on their door to make sure she was okay.

When Chasseur finished his talk, Melinda opened the program for questions from the audience.

A man stood. "This may be off the topic," he said, "but most of us are confused about what's going on here. We know that a fake murder was supposed to take place on the stage, but the consensus seems to be that it wasn't a fake after all. These police officers guarding every exit are real. That's for sure. And that detective—what's his name?—Ladd?—he's been questioning every one of us. I don't believe he's part of the show, either. So, what's going on? I think we deserve to know."

The four of us on the dais looked at each other to see who had an answer for him. Melinda tried to change the subject. "That's a question we can discuss another time," she said into her microphone. "Right now, I'd appreciate questions for our distinguished panelists about their books."

A woman got to her feet. "My question is for Mrs. Fletcher," she said. "What Mr. Chasseur said is true. We've all heard about how many real murders you've solved over the course of your career. Because we believe that the young man who was shot on stage was *really* shot and killed, I'd like to know what inroads you and the police have been making."

"Jessica?" Melinda said.

I was faced with an ethical dilemma. Earlier, there had been genuine confusion about what had happened to Paul Brody on the stage during the first act, and I wasn't uncomfortable fudging my answers to questions about whether he had, in fact, been killed. I also didn't want to betray the trust Detective Ladd had placed in me by saying anything that might hinder his investigation.

But it was now obvious to me that the actual murder could no longer be kept under wraps, and I didn't want to continue to perpetuate a lie with good people who had paid money to enjoy a strictly fictional murder mystery. I looked to Detective Ladd, who'd been joined by Mark Egmon. A few seconds of conversation ensued between them before they came to the front of the room. Ladd appeared uneasy facing a large group. He avoided eye contact and shifted from one foot to the other. Egmon, on the other hand, seemed supremely confident. He flashed a wide smile, held up his hands, and said, "I hate to interrupt this excellent panel of distinguished writers, but your questions lead me to believe that you have more on your minds than how these authors turn out such wonderful books." He turned to the dais. "Sorry, Melinda, but we've decided it's time to level with the folks."

"Finally!" someone said.

"I'll leave it to Detective Ladd to provide the specifics, at least to the extent he can. But let me say something first on behalf of Mohawk House. Our foremost concern is, and has always been, the comfort, and especially the safety, of our guests. We bend over backwards to ensure that your stay with us is pleasurable and memorable. But there are times when things happen that are beyond our control, and this unfortunate situation certainly qualifies as one of those times." He turned to Ladd. "Care to take it from here, Detective?"

"I suppose so," Ladd said, clearing his throat a few times before continuing. "Yup, the young actor named Paul Brody is dead. He was supposed to die in the play, and actually died in real life. We're investigating his death."

There were a few gasps from the audience, and a buzz as people voiced their reactions to the news. A number of them busily made notes, as though this revelation could be used to solve the murder presented in the play.

"You mean it might have been an accident and not murder?" said one man, sounding disappointed.

"All I can say is we're investigating."

The buzz grew louder as the alternative that Ladd had presented swept through the crowd. I wasn't sure he'd done the right thing. A murder had taken place. But evidently he felt that raising the possibility that the death was accidental or from natural causes might calm those susceptible to hysteria.

"Now," Ladd continued, "I know that this is bound to be pretty upsetting to you folks, especially since you came here for a fun weekend and didn't bargain on bein' part of an investigation—and I apologize for any inconvenience you might be experiencing. Can't be helped, though, and I appreciate how cooperative most of you have been. Of course, I figure no one was going anywhere anyway, not with this snowstorm we've had. But there's good news on that score. The plows are scheduled to get up here any minute now. Once they do their job, everybody will be free to pack up and leave, at least those folks I've already questioned. But I think Mr. Egmon has something to say in that regard.''

Mark announced that for those who stayed for the rest of the planned events, ten percent would be deducted from their final bill, prompting vigorous applause. *A smart move,* I thought. Keeping even a few people from defecting and demanding a full refund would more than offset money lost through the discount.

"Now," Mark said, "my suggestion—and Detective Ladd concurs—is that we let the police go about their business, cooperate with them, and enjoy the rest of the weekend. You still have a mystery to solve," he said, sweeping a hand toward Melinda.

He and Ladd started to walk away, but a woman wearing a large white straw hat stood and said loudly, "Easy enough for you to say that, sir, but what about us? You haven't apprehended the murderer, which means he might strike again at any time. Who's going to protect *us*?"

"Maybe it was a woman," said a man, followed by a hearty laugh. "Who's going to protect me from some bloodthirsty female?"

His comment elicited giggles, and everyone started conferring with their teammates.

Amazing, I thought, *how quickly moods can change.* Was it Mark Egmon's announcement that ten percent of their bills would be waived that elevated their spirits? Or was it the challenge of actually being so close to a real murder mystery, as opposed to the literary ones they were used to reading? No matter what had caused it, there was a marked excitement in the room that certainly hadn't been there during our abbreviated session.

I stood, assuming that the panel discussion was over. But Chasseur pulled his microphone close and said, "If I could please have your attention." He repeated it twice more, until conversations ebbed. "I know," he continued, "that Mrs. Fletcher has this reputation of being a super detective, besides writing about murder. But in this case, I'm afraid she's about to be outdone by yours truly."

His statement brought a further hush to the room.

"I've been working closely with Detective Ladd and his men," he said, flashing a diabolical grin at the police officer. "In fact, I've already offered the police my take on what might have occurred, and I intend to continue delving into the matter until the murderer—and it *was* a murder—is exposed and brought to justice. I tell you this because I want, and need, your help. The local press will be arriving right after the snowplows, and my publicist has arranged for national media to be involved, too. What I want to do is work with you on solving this crime. How about this? We split up into three teams. I'll lead one, and Jessica Fletcher and GSB Wick will lead the other two. You can keep working with your original teams to solve the murder in the play. But we'll also work together to solve the real murder that's taken place.

It'll make for a great story—noted mystery writers band together with devoted mystery lovers to bring a criminal to justice."

A number of people affirmed with whoops, hollers, and applause. I looked to the rear of the room where Ladd and Egmon stood, their expressions very much at odds with the sentiments of the audience.

Chasseur turned to Georgie and me. "Up to the challenge, ladies?" he asked.

"I think this is totally inappropriate," I said.

"I agree with Jessica," said Georgie.

"Suit yourselves," Chasseur said. He spoke into the microphone again. "One of the reasons we're here," he announced, "is to sign books. I'll be in the gift shop, pen in hand. See you there."

Chasseur left the room, with a group of fans trailing behind him.

"The nerve," Georgie said.

"He's not without ego," I said, "and a flair for self-promotion. Nothing will come of it."

Other members of the audience encircled us at the dais.

"I'd like to be on your team, Mrs. Fletcher," some people said.

"I'll bet you win," said others to Georgie.

"Ah don't think there's anything to win," she responded softly.

"I'm afraid Ms. Wick and I don't agree with what Mr. Chasseur has suggested," I said. "But you're free to join with him if you wish."

I saw in their faces disappointment at the stance

I'd taken. This weekend of an interactive theatrical murder mystery had now taken on an entirely new dimension. Chasseur had offered them a bonus, a chance to work closely with an established writer to actually investigate and solve a real murder. Egmon probably could have saved the hotel the ten percent rebate if he'd known how excited the guests would be about this new wrinkle in their weekend experience. I seriously doubted if any of them would opt to leave early. I heard one of them say to another as they turned to leave, "She isn't very friendly, is she?"

"Too stuck up to join in," said her friend.

I didn't have time to feel the sting of their comments because Egmon and Ladd came to the dais.

"Did you know he was going to do that?" Mark asked.

"Absolutely not," I said. "Georgie and I don't want any part of it."

"Good," Ladd said. "Maybe the whole stupid thing will just die a natural death."

"In the meantime," Mark said, "you two ladies have books to sign."

"Right," I said.

"Ah'd better check on Harold," Georgie said. "Ah'll join y'all in a few minutes."

Mark walked me to the gift shop. We were almost there when Larry Savoy intercepted me. "I heard what John did," he said. "I can't believe it."

"Well, you'd better," I said.

"I'll make sure he mentions the troupe. This'll plaster our names across the country," Larry said. "I couldn't ask for better publicity." He rubbed his hands together and hustled into the gift store, pushing aside people on the line to get up front to where Chasseur was autographing books.

"Maybe he has a point," Egmon said. "I wonder if the publicity will help or hurt us. For sure, we'd better plan on another mystery weekend next year."

I sighed.

"Oh, Jessica, you wanted me to open one of the doors on the third floor." He pulled out a ring of keys

"That's right," I said.

"Want to go now?"

"Why don't we wait until after I sign books?" To myself, I added, *If people still want Jessica Fletcher's signature even if she won't participate in this farce of an investigation Chasseur planned.*

Mark put the keys back in his pocket. "Sure. I'll be in my office all afternoon getting ready for the press. I don't know why Chasseur pulled a stunt like this. I hope it doesn't backfire on us."

I smiled and patted his arm. "No one's going to blame the hotel," I said. "And maybe Larry is right. The publicity could be helpful."

Larry emerged from the crowd standing in line, books in hand, waiting for their turn with Chasseur, and they hoped, Georgie and me. "I've got to get to rehearsal," he said. "The next scene is pretty rough."

"It'll be a standing-room-only crowd, judging from their reaction to the last performance," I said. "Larry, do you have a bio of Paul Brody?"

"Bio? Sure. I have a bio for every actor, and plenty of head shots, too. Why?"

"I'd like to know more about him, his past, his career, anything at all."

"Swing by the auditorium after the signing. I'll put it aside for you."

The gift shop manager had set up three small tables, with a pile of the appropriate books in front of each author. Chasseur's bravado announcement had paid off for him; the line to purchase a signed book from him was considerably longer than those for Georgie and me. I kept waiting for her to return as I chatted pleasantly with the book-buying guests and personally inscribed the books they purchased.

"Where's Ms. Wick?" a woman asked. "I'm her biggest fan."

"She had to tend to a personal matter," I said, "but I'm sure she'll be along any minute."

It wasn't until I'd signed my last book and was preparing to leave to go to Mark Egmon's office that Georgie entered the shop. With her was Harold Boynton. A wave of relief swept over me. I had expected her to announce that he'd had a heart attack. He looked a lot better than he had at lunch. It was Georgie who appeared to be ill now. I didn't know whether she'd actually seen Paul Brody's spirit, or for that matter any one of the ghosts she was fond of writing about, but she certainly looked as though she had.

"Feeling better?" I asked Boynton."

"Yes, quite. Thank you for asking."

"Are you all right?" I asked Georgie as she settled behind her table and uncapped a pen.

"I don't know," she said, greeting the first buyer in her line and managing a smile.

I glanced up at Boynton, who stood behind us. His eyes darted right and left before he bent over and whispered in my ear, "I saw him."

I turned in my chair. "Who did you see?" I asked.

"The dead actor."

"Paul Brody?"

"Yes."

Chasseur was still signing books and chatting with buyers. My line had dried up completely. I stood and said to Boynton, "Let's go outside."

We went into the hall and to an alcove. I stood with my back to the wall. He stood too close to me, his large belly pressing against my arm. He breathed heavily, and I smelled alcohol on his breath. I managed to slide to my right, providing a little distance between us. "Now," I said, "tell me about seeing Paul Brody."

"It's a long story. I don't know where to begin."

"Try the beginning," I said, not eager to prolong the conversation.

"Ah, yes," he said. "You Americans like to get to the point. No dillydallying."

"Yes. We're very direct."

"I will try to accommodate you. As you know, I wasn't feeling well after my altercation with Mr. Chasseur."

"Did the food make you ill?"

"I might have overindulged a bit. The plat du jour was absolutely superb. But I felt better after lying down for a while, and when I got up I treated myself to a taste of a fine single-malt scotch. I always carry it with me in a traveling flask. I think it aids digestion. In any case, it positively aids disposition." He laughed at his own joke, but seeing no smile on my face, sobered his expression and cleared his throat. "Anyway, I grew restless waiting for Georgie to return and decided to take a walk. Not a long one, mind you. I still wasn't feeling tip-top."

"Where did you go?"

"Just about the hotel. Fascinating place, isn't it? Lots of bloody history within these walls." A chuckle. "Bloody in more ways than one."

I sighed and glanced at my watch. "I don't mean to be rude, but I have someplace to be, Mr. Boynton. Please tell me what you saw during your walk."

"Oh, yes, right-o. I decided to stroll upstairs where Georgie said she'd seen the dead chap, up on the third floor. And there he was."

"Where?"

"In the corridor. Oh, I tell you, when he saw me round the bend, he skedaddled away. That's what you Americans would say, isn't it? Well, that's what he did. Disappeared into one of those rooms up there just where Georgie said she'd seen him."

"Which one of the rooms?" I asked.

He gave me the number. "Knocked on the door, but got no answer. Not surprised, though."

"You're sure it was Brody?"

"Well, I—I think it was. I might be getting on in years, but my eyesight is still bloody good, like a man half my age." He leered. "My eyesight is not the only thing that hasn't aged, Jessica."

"You're saying it was the actor, not a ghost?" I persisted.

"Unlike my esteemed friend Georgie, I don't believe in ghosts. I've seen a lot of dead men in my life, Jessica, my dear. I may call you Jessica, may I not? And I think I can tell the difference between dead and alive. And this body was definitely alive." He fingered the collar of my sweater.

I thanked him for confiding in me and moved away as quickly as I could, but not fast enough. He grabbed my hand. "It would be my pleasure to buy the lovely Jessica Fletcher a drink," he said, stroking my fingers and peering into my eyes.

"You're too kind," I said, "but I'm afraid there's no time." I extricated my hand from his. "I must run. I'll see you and Georgie at dinner."

I left him standing in the hall and headed back in the direction of the gift shop. Chasseur was still surrounded by fans. Georgie had only two people in her line—Sydney Pomerantz, the man Detective Ladd suspected of strangling his first wife, and the redheaded Ms. Carlisle.

As I proceeded to Mark Egmon's office, I tried to make sense out of what I'd just heard from Harold Boynton. Had what he claimed to have seen been an alcoholic vision? Maybe he was so influenced by Georgie and her purported sighting of Paul Brody that he, too, imagined seeing him. Or was he using Georgie's story for himself, to get closer to me? I shuddered at this last possibility.

But why he and Georgie had made their bizarre claims really didn't matter. There were more worldly avenues to pursue in going after Brody's murderer, and I intended to follow up every one of them. Chasseur had thrown down the gauntlet, and while I had no interest in competing with him—or anyone else, for that matter—I was determined to get to the bottom of things—even if it killed me.

Chapter Nineteen

Some mystery writers make good use of history in their novels. One introduced to readers a medieval monk, Brother Cadfael, who dabbled in solving crimes. Name this author.

Before going to Mark Egmon's office, I swung by the auditorium, where Larry Savoy was rehearsing the next scene.

"I still can't believe Chasseur pulled that dumb trick," he said, "announcing Paul's murder."

"And becoming very popular in the bargain," I said. "You promised me a copy of Paul's bio."

"Right."

He called to Melinda, who was blocking a bit of stage action for Monroe and Victoria Whittaker, and asked for the bio. She rummaged through a large briefcase and found it. "Here you go," she said, handing the bio to Larry, who passed it to me. I folded it and put it in the pocket of my sweater.

"Don't believe everything you read on it, Jessica," Larry cautioned. "Actors and actresses have a habit of embellishing their résumés."

"Like many people," I said. "I read someplace that thirty percent of people looking for jobs exaggerate or downright lie on their résumés. Did you check Paul's references?"

He laughed. "Who has time for that?" he said.

"I'll leave you to your rehearsal," I said. "Thanks for the bio."

Mark Egmon was on his way out the door when I arrived at his office. "Oh, Jessica," he said, "I'm afraid I can't go with you right now. The storm brought down a couple of big trees across the access road. They're on our property and the plows can't get up here until we clear them. I'm on my way to a meeting with the grounds super."

"That's all right," I said. "You go to your meeting and I'll—"

"No, no," he said. "Wait. I'll get you the pass-keys." He popped back into his office and returned with a large ring holding dozens of keys. He went through them until he found the one he wanted and handed the ring to me by that key. "This is the one for that door up in the VIP section of the third floor. Be my guest." He grinned. "You're now holding the keys to every room in the hotel. Lucky for me you're not a robber. Just drop them on my desk when you're through."

"Are you sure you won't need these?"

"No problem. Have to run. Just don't lock yourself in up there. Could take a week to find you." He was gone, his laugh trailing behind.

I would have preferred that Mark accompany me, but I understood that he had other priorities at that moment. As I waited for an elevator to arrive, I looked down at the ring of keys and stifled a sense of discomfort at holding the keys to the hotel's inner recesses, almost as though I were embarking on an illicit act. Silly, of course. He'd willingly given me the keys and encouraged me to explore on my own. Still . . .

The elevator arrived. I got in, pressed the button for the third floor, and was soon standing in front of the three VIP suites. Although I was alone—the housemaids had probably finished tidying up that section of the hotel and were performing their duties elsewhere—I had the feeling I was being watched. Was someone observing me from one of the suites through the peephole in the door? I glanced around for a surveillance camera but saw none. I knew that this portion of the building was part of the original Mohawk House where the earl had lived and died. I've always loved old buildings with historic significance, although when it comes to choosing hotels in my travels, I find myself increasingly drawn to newer ones with more up-to-date amenities, charm failing to compensate for faulty plumbing and balky air-conditioning. It comes with age, I suppose.

I turned in a circle and tried to visualize what it was like living in Mohawk House generations ago. Had the earl been married? Did he have children? How many servants catered to his wishes? Did he entertain lavishly, or live in relative seclusion, rattling around his mansion until that fateful night when someone separated his head from his body as he slept? Maybe I'd learn more about him one day, I told myself as I looked at the three doors leading into the suites, and the fourth, smaller door, not a guest room, that was locked, the key to which I held in my hand.

I looked at the other keys on the ring. Mark had said that the ring held keys to every room in the hotel. Curiosity can be a powerful compulsion, rivaling smoking, drinking, gambling, and other addictions. Was the answer to Paul Brody's murder contained in one of the suites? Probably not, but I've always operated under the leave-no-stone-unturned theory. A closed door, including that fourth one, never fails to pique my curiosity.

As I started toward it, the door to the middle suite opened. "Mrs. Fletcher," Sydney Pomerantz said. His wife came to his side. They'd changed into matching red vests with gold buttons over white turtlenecks.

"Hello," I said.

"Looking for someone?" he asked, eyeing my fistful of keys.

"No, not exactly," I said, hoping they were on their way out.

"That's quite a lot of keys you have," he said, the space between *keys* and *you* filled by a *glunk* from his throat.

"Yes, it is," I said, hoping they wouldn't ask more questions. "Are you enjoying yourselves this weekend?"

"Very much," said Mrs. Pomerantz, who had blue-white hair and a pink face remarkably unlined considering her age. "It was quite a shock to hear Mr. Chasseur say that precious young actor was brutally murdered." She shuddered. "Gives me the chills."

"Fortunately," I said, trying to stuff the large key ring in my small pocket, "the police have the situation well in hand."

"Oh, don't count on that," Mr. Pomerantz said. "I've lived here for many years and know firsthand how inept they are. Take it from me. I have experience."

I didn't acknowledge that I knew what he was talking about.

"Well, nice seeing you again," I said. It seemed to me that they weren't about to move. But they did, closing the door behind them and starting down the hall.

"Oh, by the way," I said. They stopped and turned. "Do you know Ms. Carlisle, the woman who has the suite next to you?"

They looked at each other, their expressions clearly saying that they weren't fond of their neighbor.

"Do you know anything about her?" I asked.

"Just that she's a very rude lady," Mrs. Pomerantz said. "Doesn't even say good morning to me."

"I think she's part of the play," Mr. Pomerantz said.

"Yes, I've heard that, too," I said. "Have you seen a young man in this hallway who might look like the actor who was killed?"

Another look at each other before he said, "Can't

say that we have, but we've heard noises out here in the hall in the middle of the night."

"What sort of noises?"

"Enough to wake us," said the wife.

"Heard people arguing," he said.

"A man?"

"Man and a woman. You know, Mrs. Fletcher, you might want to find some time to meet with me. I have a lot of experience with forensic science and police procedures. I'd be happy to share what I know with you for one of your books."

"That's kind of you," I said.

"Just name the time (glunk) and place. By the way, I've been doing some investigating of my own since the actor was killed."

"Oh?"

"That's right. The way I see it, the murderer is a member of the hotel staff, possibly a kitchen worker with access to weapons, knives, cleavers, that sort of thing."

"Interesting conclusion," I said.

They walked away, and I decided I'd better stop standing around in the hall. I went to the door and inserted the key Mark Egmon had identified for me. It turned easily. I pushed the door open and stepped inside. Were it not for the dim light coming from what appeared to be a window at the distant end of a corridor, it would have been pitch-black. The ceiling was low, necessitating my crouching to avoid hitting my head. Was this passageway used by the earl's servants? It was customary in years gone by for household help to remain out of sight as much as possible, and I knew that houses of this vintage often provided ways for the staff to move throughout them without encountering the owners and their guests. *Servants were shorter in those days,* I thought.

I gently closed the door, careful not to allow the latch to engage fully and lock behind me.

A flashlight would have come in handy, but mine was in my shoulder bag, hanging in the closet of my room. Its lack, however, wasn't cause to abandon my plan. I briefly considered getting down on my hands and knees to avoid straining my back, but I didn't want to ruin my hose. Instead, I hunched over and started toward the window, which I judged was forty or fifty feet away. It was slow going, and dirty. Years of dust and dirt adhered to the walls and covered the floor, my footsteps kicking it up and fouling the air. My short journey seemed to take forever, and I was happy to reach the window, as the ceiling was higher there, allowing me to straighten a bit and ease the kinks in my back and shoulders. I couldn't tell what the window overlooked because its panes were covered with decades of thick grime.

The low, narrow corridor took a left turn at the window and continued toward what appeared to be another window. I considered going back. I had no idea what I was looking for. But something told me that Paul Brody's killer might have discovered these passageways and used one to flee the murder scene

and blend back in with the hotel's paying guests, the
theatrical troupe, and the staff.

I set off on the next leg and reached that second
window. There was yet another length of corridor,
this one with light at the far end that didn't seem to
emanate from a window. It was brighter than that—
an artificial light. Grimacing against the strain in my
back and shoulders, I forged ahead until I emerged
in a wide room with a ceiling almost as low as the
paths leading to it, although I was able to stand, the
hair on the top of my head brushing the ceiling.
Squares of opaque glass, illuminated from below,
were inserted in the wooden floor, which was littered
with coiled wires and disks of tinted acetate, red,
green, yellow, and blue. The windowless room was
stuffy and warm, as if no air from outside ever
reached it.

As I adjusted to my new surroundings, I heard
voices and tried to ascertain where they were coming
from. They were below me, I decided.

*"Really, Victoria. I can't believe you knew the young
man's father,"* a muffled voice said.

The play! I was hearing the rehearsal of the next
scene of Larry and Melinda's production, which
meant I was standing in a space above the auditorium. The wires and filters must have been for the
stage lighting at some point. But what had this room
been used for in bygone days? Was it still used now?
Given the layers of dust, I doubted it. It must have
been abandoned as too difficult to reach.

I looked for another access. *There must be one different from the route I took*, I thought, picking my way across the room carefully, avoiding the glass panels, fearing to tread on any rotten boards, and conscious that I'd just as soon the actors on the stage below me not become aware of anyone creeping around over their heads. As I progressed along the length of the room, the voices from below became louder. I paused a few times to take in what they were saying and could clearly hear the actors and actresses reciting their lines. At the far end of the room, their voices grew inaudible again—*I must be over the backstage area now*, I thought—and there was a door. I went to it and turned the knob. It opened and I stepped into yet another passageway, this one with a ceiling that accommodated my full height. I saw a light switch and flipped it up. A few wall sconces came to life. Splendid! I could stand up straight, and see, too.

The hallway ended abruptly, with no apparent exit, but when I looked down, I saw what appeared to be a trapdoor in the floor. I crouched and pushed on it. A hinge with a spring made moving the trapdoor difficult, but I managed to crack it open enough to see what was below. It was that same area Larry and I had discovered after going through the door in the wardrobe room, the place where my pushing on the bar of a door leading to a small terrace had summoned hotel security guards.

I now knew that the area of the third floor in which the three VIP suites were located was connected with the spot on which I currently stood, making it possible that whoever stabbed Paul Brody could have made his, or her, escape through the passageways I'd just traveled. Not that there was anything concrete to prove that it had happened that way. But at least I now knew it was physically possible.

I released the trapdoor, stood up again, and became aware of an odor I hadn't detected before. It was the acrid smell of smoke, cigarette smoke. Had it been there before? Was I so absorbed in my investigation of the secret passages in the hotel that my other senses had ceased to be perceptive? My eyesight isn't what it was in my youth but my sense of smell has always been acute. I'm often aware of an aroma before others become conscious of it.

Could someone backstage be smoking? It was unlikely. I'd heard Larry and Melinda warn the cast and crew about the hotel's no-smoking policy. I inhaled three or four times, turning my head as I did to determine where the smoke originated. Since I was at a dead end, unless one went down through the trapdoor, whoever was smoking had to be behind me, and the only thing behind me was the room over the stage and auditorium. Although it was uncomfortably warm where I stood, I felt a sudden chill. It wasn't caused by someone smoking a cigarette where he or she shouldn't have been. It was caused by my suspicion that someone had followed me on my doubled-over journey through the passageways.

I turned around in the short hallway, searching the immediate vicinity for something to use in the event I needed protection, but came up empty-handed. I strained to hear better, but only an eerie silence reached my ears. I knew I couldn't simply continue to stand there. Was the trapdoor an option? I thought not. Even if I could manage to hold it fully open and squeeze through at the same time, I didn't relish falling to the floor underneath it.

Drawing a few deep breaths for fortitude, I began my return journey, ever alert for a sound or other sign of an unwanted presence. I reached the opening to the large room and paused there. The smell of a burning cigarette was more pronounced now. With one final deep breath, which I held, I stepped into the room, my eyes scanning the space in a wide arc. I exhaled noisily. I was alone. Whoever had been there was gone.

I contemplated seeing if I could catch up with my pursuer, but decided against it. By the time I reached the fourth door on the third floor, he or she would have had ample time to disappear from sight, either into one of the VIP suites or down a stairwell to another floor.

I stood silently, listening to the rehearsal in progress below. The actors were running through a scene in which Catarina, the maid, admitted that she'd had an affair with Paul in New York, and had come to the Whittaker home to sabotage his new romance with Cynthia—just as Larry said it was written in the script. But he'd also said the script mirrored reality; the actress had been dumped unceremoniously by Paul in real life. Had Larry passed that same infor-

mation along to Detective Ladd? I made a mental
note to ask.

Catarina had been speaking. Now, suddenly, I
heard Larry's loud voice: "Stop! Enough! Really, Catarina, can you please bring your voice down an oc-
tave?" He mimicked her high-pitched way of speaking,
using a falsetto voice of his own. I had to smile. His
impression of Catarina was excellent; he sounded just
like her.

The actors began rehearsing the scene once more,
and I prepared to retrace my steps back to the VIP
suites. Looking down as I traversed the cluttered
floor, I spotted a partially consumed cigarette on the
dusty boards. I picked it up and examined it closely.
It had been crushed out, but it didn't look like this
butt had been discarded years ago. The paper was
still supple and the shreds of tobacco that clung to
it were fresh. I turned it over. It was the same brand
as one of the cigarettes I'd found in the vestibule
where I'd first encountered Paul Brody, and the same
brand that had been on my balcony the night I got
locked out of the room. I wrapped it in a tissue and
braced for the painful trip through the low-ceilinged
passageways. But I hadn't gone more than a few feet
when something else caught my eye. I stared down
at it. On the floor was a tool of some sort, with a
wooden handle and a long, round, slender blade
about five inches long. I took an even closer look.
No doubt about it; that was blood on the blade.

I pulled a handkerchief from my pocket and used

it to gingerly pick up the blade. I remembered the stagehand, Jeremy, asking whether anyone had seen his pick. Was this the pick to which he was referring? "Pick" seemed an appropriate word to describe it.

Holding the pick in one hand, I bent over and eventually made my way back to door leading to the third-floor VIP suites. As I reached for the knob, I realized the door was now fully closed. I'd left it ajar. *Not again!* I thought as I turned the knob. Much to my relief, the door opened and I was alone in the hallway.

The door to the Pomerantz suite was closed, as were the others. I stepped close to the suite occupied by Ms. Carlisle and pressed my ear against its door. There was no sound on the other side. I impetuously wrapped my free hand around the knob and turned. It opened.

"Hello," I said softly. I wrinkled my nose. The heavy, unpleasant odor of cigarette smoke assaulted my nostrils. Evidently, Ms. Carlisle wasn't someone who followed no-smoking rules. It smelled as though she'd smoked heavily, the smoke permeating everything in the room, couches and chairs, drapes and carpeting.

The noise of the elevator doors opening came from down the hall. I quickly closed the door and assumed a nonchalant posture. Coming toward me was Ms. Carlisle. "Good afternoon," I said pleasantly, holding my handkerchief containing the pick behind my thigh.

"Good afternoon to you, dearie," she said, passing me. I watched her reach the door to her suite, open it, and disappear inside, the door slamming behind her.

I was about to leave the area when the door to the third suite opened, the one not occupied by Ms. Carlisle or Mr. and Mrs. Pomerantz. Jeremy, the lead stagehand, stepped into the hall.

"Hello," I said.

"Hi," he muttered, and walked quickly away, overtly uneasy for some reason. As he moved down the hall almost at a trot, it occurred to me that he could easily be mistaken for the deceased Paul Brody, particularly in a low-light, fleeting situation. Jeremy was about the same height as Paul, although he was more muscular. Was he staying in that third suite? It seemed unlikely that a stagehand would be given one of the best rooms in the hotel while the Savoys were in a lesser room. Had Georgie Wick and Harold Boynton seen Jeremy and thought he was Paul? It certainly was a possibility. I looked at the bloody weapon secured in my handkerchief. I could have asked Jeremy whether it was what he'd been looking for, but was glad I hadn't. I would turn it over directly to Detective Ladd.

I came downstairs to where the older gentleman at the desk was reading a magazine. He looked up and greeted me.

"What's new with the storm?" I asked.

He mentioned the downed trees.

"Yes," I said, "Mark Egmon told me about it."

I went to the main entrance and took a look outside. The snow had stopped, but the huge drifts that had been blown against the building were still there. Two cops in uniform leaned against the wall, appearing to be on the verge of falling asleep standing up.

"Shouldn't be long," I said.

"Better not be," one replied.

I found Ladd in the room Mark Egmon had provided him for his investigation and handed him the pick.

"Where'd you get this?" he asked.

I explained.

"Has to be the murder weapon," he said.

"I'd say that's a safe assumption."

"Let's keep this between us," he said.

"I wouldn't have it any other way," I said.

I went to my room, added my most recent cigarette butt to the others I'd amassed, pulled out Paul Brody's bio, and started to read. His list of acting credits was long, segregated into parts he'd played in theater, on television, and in feature films. I remembered what Larry had said, that actors sometimes embellish their résumés. Was that the case here? Nothing on the page made me sit up and take notice, so I tossed the bio on the desk, went to the French doors, and looked outside. The sky had lightened a bit, although some lingering flakes still fell.

I grabbed my room key from where I'd laid it on the desk and left. But I'd taken only a few steps toward the staircase when it hit me. I returned to the room and looked at Paul Brody's bio again. One of the films he'd listed as having appeared in was *Murder by Special Delivery*, the film Claudette Chasseur said she'd acted in, the one coproduced by her husband, John.

Chapter Twenty

What was Ed McBain's real name?

I ran the ring of keys back to Mark Egmon's office—
I was told by a secretary that he was at another
meeting—and returned to my room.

I'm an inveterate note-maker, sometimes to the
amusement of my friends back home. I always justify
it by pointing to airline pilots as an example. No
matter how many thousands of flying hours a commercial pilot might have, he or she wouldn't dream
of taking off without first going through an elaborate
checklist. My friends usually retort that I'm not an
airline pilot. But that isn't the point. It's too easy to
forget important things in a busy life, and my notes
make that less of a possibility.

But there's more behind my penchant for making
notes than not wanting to miss an appointment or
forget an item in the supermarket. Writing things
down helps organize thoughts. I've always been a
firm believer in that, and stressed it back when I was
an English teacher. Ideas, questions, conceptions, and
answers float around in our brains, sometimes collid-

ing, too often becoming lost. By committing them to paper, we can create a structure that helps prevent this from happening. Maybe I need written notes because I'm internally disorganized. Maybe others are internally organized to the extent that they don't need written reminders of what they're thinking. No matter. I'm a note-maker.

It was evident to me that Paul Brody's murderer came from one of three groups at Mohawk House that weekend.

The most likely source was the cast and crew of the Savoys' theatrical troupe. The problem was that I hadn't had the opportunity to interact with them very much. I made a note to try to correct that.

The second group was the hundred or so paying guests; they could not be summarily ruled out. Detective Ladd had been systematically questioning them, but I had no knowledge as to what information his questions had elicited. Had one of them attended the weekend at Mohawk House with the specific intention of stabbing Paul Brody to death? If the murderer came from that contingent, it was up to Detective Ladd to ferret out the culprit. I hadn't had a chance to spend much time with the guests beyond just passing pleasantries. Sydney Pomerantz was intriguing, of course, based upon what Detective Ladd had told me about him, but I wasn't interested at that juncture with his past. The here and now was of much greater concern.

Group number three comprised my fellow writers and those accompanying them. While I wouldn't initially have considered them likely suspects, my perception had changed once I'd gotten to know them.

Another gap in my knowledge had to do with the deceased, Paul Brody. According to others, he was a difficult person whose attitude problems had caused him considerable trouble in Hollywood and possibly had derailed his aspirations to become a film star. *Question:* Why hadn't John Chasseur or his wife, Claudette, mentioned that Brody had been in a film produced by Chasseur, in which Claudette had a role? Surely they hadn't forgotten him. I thought back to what Chasseur had said—that Brody's murderer was undoubtedly a woman who'd been burned by him. Was he dropping a hint about his own wife? I couldn't come up with a reason at that moment why he might do such a thing, unless . . . unless it was to deflect suspicion from *him*. From what I knew of Chasseur, his ethical and moral compasses weren't especially steady, and his allegiance to his wife was, from what I'd observed, nonexistent.

When Brody and his brother were young, they had accompanied their mother and father to Mohawk House and had explored the hidden recesses of the historic mansion. Did that play a part in Paul's demise? My explorations had established only that it was possible for the killer to have made use of those hidden areas as a means of escape, and as a place in which to discard the murder weapon. Their father had been a producer, primarily for the stage but with some Hollywood involvement. Were the parents still alive? What was their relationship with the adult

Paul? I made another note to see what I could learn in that regard.

Larry Savoy had told me that Brody would have been fired from the troupe once the Mohawk House weekend was over. Did Brody know that? Larry had also indicated that Brody was causing trouble for him with the actors union. Motive to have killed the actor? Shaky, but murders have been committed for lesser reasons than that.

Melinda Savoy, according to Larry, had lobbied for Brody to be part of the cast. Had she been involved with the dead actor in some sort of romantic relationship? I heard Larry and Melinda arguing. Was it about Brody?

According to Larry, Catarina had had an affair with Brody in New York City and had been unceremoniously discarded by him. In the script, she'd come to work for the Whittakers in order to be near him, and to interfere in his new relationship with Cynthia Whittaker. Had she auditioned for the cast in order to be near him in real life and perhaps exact her revenge for the way he'd treated her?

What about GSB "Georgie" Wick? As much as I admired her as a writer, and liked her as a person, I would be less than candid not to acknowledge that she was "strange." Not that "strange" people necessarily go around killing others. But Georgie certainly had a problem with separating fact from fiction. She'd been in love with a young man who, I surmised, had died prematurely. He looked like Brody, she'd told me, and she claimed that he still visited her, bearing flowers. Had she imagined that Paul Brody was her deceased former lover and stabbed him to death while in some sort of delusional state?

Georgie's friend, Harold Boynton, could hardly be considered a viable suspect. But both he and Georgie claimed to have seen Brody very much alive after the actor had been stabbed to death. Was Boynton, who'd spent his adult years cavorting around a morgue surrounded by dead bodies, mentally unbalanced? He didn't come across that way to me, but then again I hardly knew him.

That left other members of the cast aside from Catarina and the Savoys.

Cynthia Whittaker had complained about Brody groping her. But her reaction at the cast meeting conveyed something else. Laura Tehaar, the young woman in charge of props, had displayed overt affection for Brody at that cast meeting.

Monroe Whittaker, the veteran actor who played the father, disliked Brody, according to the script. But what were his views of him off the stage? The same question held for Victoria Whittaker. She seemed to know quite a bit about the deceased. She knew his real age and was aware of his failed Hollywood career. Had she known Brody in Hollywood, perhaps been involved with him romantically?

There was also Ms. Carlisle, the redheaded lady who was part of the Savoy troupe. It was hard to gauge her because I'd had so little interaction with her. She'd not appeared onstage, at least not yet. What was her theatrical background? Had she known

Brody from previous show business adventures? Had she been the woman arguing with Brody the first night at the hotel when I came in out of the cold and found him there? Had he been smoking? He'd quit, according to Larry Savoy, but that didn't mean he wasn't sneaking a smoke now and then. Ms. Carisle certainly was a heavy smoker, based upon the odor emanating from her suite.

My thoughts kept coming back to Chasseur and his wife. According to Larry, Chasseur had lobbied hard to be part of the weekend, and jumped at the chance when another writer, Tony Tedeschi, dropped out for personal reasons. Chasseur had wanted to be there, yet seemed disinterested in the event and his role in it. Why?

Who'd followed me through that fourth door on the third floor? Whoever it was had been smoking a cigarette. *No, wait*, I told myself. A cigarette had been lighted, but that didn't mean the person was actually smoking it. Did the man or woman following me want to implicate someone else who was known to be a cigarette smoker?

What was the stagehand, Jeremy, doing in one of the third-floor VIP suites? I knew nothing of him except that he resembled Brody to some extent. Had he and Brody been vying for the attentions of the same woman, leading to a fatal altercation between them? I had nothing upon which to base that, but I wrote it down anyway. So many possibilities, so few answers.

I capped my pen, sat back, closed my eyes and

pondered the notes I'd made. The reason there were too few answers to the many questions I'd noted was that I hadn't been actively seeking them by speaking with the right people.

I opened my eyes. Two hours until dinner. I freshened up in the bathroom, slipped my notepad and pen into my pocket, and headed for the auditorium, where I hoped the rehearsal would still be in progress. The snow had stopped. Soon the road down the mountain would be clear, and everyone would be leaving, including Paul Brody's killer.

I couldn't let that happen.

Chapter Twenty-one

The popular TV show **Diagnosis Murder,** *which starred Dick Van Dyke, has been resurrected in a series of original novels.*
Who writes them?
(Hint: He used to be the TV show's executive producer and writer.)

I was on my way to the auditorium when I made a sudden change in plans. I went to Mark Egmon's office and found that he'd just returned from his latest meeting.

"Mark, I was wondering whether you have a spare computer I could use to go online. I usually travel with my laptop but left it home this trip."

"Sure. No problem. Looking for something specific?"

"Anything about Paul Brody. I've read his bio, but he might have a Web site that would provide additional information."

He led me into a small, spartan room off his office that contained a computer, a desk, a chair, and not much else. "Make yourself at home," he said. "This may be an old building, but the computer system is wireless. Log on to your heart's content."

He left, and I sat down in front of the monitor. I connected with Google and typed in the name *Paul Brody*. I was given a choice of 613,000 sites. I added *actor* to his name. A picture of Brody came to life, embedded in his home page's text, which began with a bio. It confirmed that he came from a theatrical family—his father a producer of Broadway shows and a few motion pictures, his mother a former ballerina. Besides being a producer, his father was also founder and head of a small pharmaceutical firm that had struck it big when a controversial cancer drug it had been developing received FDA approval. No surprise that his business success had preceded his foray into theater and film. Raising money is the primary job of a producer. Having one's own millions to invest in a play or film certainly eases the path.

Paul was born in New York City and attended private schools there before enrolling as a theater major at NYU. He dropped out after two years and studied acting with various teachers in the city, none of whose names registered with me—Stanislavsky and Adler weren't among them. The bio listed various off-Broadway shows in which he'd appeared, small roles it seemed. Then he'd left New York and moved to Los Angeles, where he pursued a motion picture career. Those credits were few; none of the films in which he'd appeared were familiar to me, their titles hinting at their subject matter: violence and sex.

One credit caught my attention, however. His most substantive role had been playing a female impersonator in a motion picture targeting the gay audience. A few reviews were included, each praising his performance.

Interesting, I thought as I continued to peruse his

credits. I would have thought after success in the gay role, he'd have found similar film parts to play, but none were listed. The bio ended by saying he'd moved to San Francisco, where he'd become a featured performer in that city's well-known female impersonator clubs.

I stopped reading, sat back and tried to reconcile the Paul Brody I'd seen at Mohawk House with the one depicted on his Web site. The Paul Brody I'd encountered appeared to be a virile, masculine man who had a reputation for pursuing women, over-aggressively, it seemed in too many cases. Of course, that didn't mean he wasn't talented enough to shift gender roles and play a woman—or a drag queen, as such performers are called.

The bio went on for three pages, complete with photographs of him in male clothing and a couple of shots of him dressed as a woman. There were additional pages, but I didn't bother to read them. An ink-jet printer was connected to the computer, and I printed out everything.

"Get what you need?" Egmon asked.

"Yes, thank you. I got exactly what I needed—I think."

"You don't sound too sure."

"I'm not sure of anything these days," I said. "Did you get the trees cleared?"

"They're working on it. Should be done by now, which means the plows will be here any minute."

I reacted to that news with mixed emotions. On the one hand, it was good that the mountain road would finally be open and people could come and go as they pleased. On the other hand, it meant that whoever killed Paul Brody would be on his or her way, perhaps never to be brought to justice. That latter possibility was unacceptable.

"Mark," I said, "I saw the fellow who works backstage coming out of one of the VIP suites upstairs. His name is Jeremy. Do you have any idea why he might have been in a suite?"

His "No" was accompanied by a shrug and "unless he roomed up there with Brody."

"Brody was in one of the suites?"

"For one night. You asked me to check where he'd been put after leaving your room. He was moved to a VIP suite until a lesser room opened up. But that third suite has been empty ever since."

"Well," I said, standing and collecting the pages from the printer, "perhaps Jeremy still has a key. Thanks for the use of the computer."

"My pleasure. Where are you off to?"

"The rehearsal. Have you spoken with Detective Ladd lately?"

"Yes. I sense that he isn't making much headway in his investigation."

"I don't wonder," I said. "There are so many people—"

"So many suspects?"

"Exactly. Thanks again."

The rehearsal was in full swing when I walked into the auditorium. Judging from the tension I sensed in the room, things weren't going well. Larry was pacing the stage in front of Monroe and Victoria Whittaker. Catarina, the maid, and the daughter, Cynthia, sat together on a couch, their faces grim. I spotted Melinda seated at the rear of the house and joined her.

"How's it going?" I asked.

"Not good," she said.

"What's the problem?"

"Larry is being unusually difficult. I mean, he's always difficult, but this time he's impossible. He's on everyone's case. You'd think he was directing an Arthur Miller or Edward Albee play on Broadway. This is supposed to be fun, broad, slapstick comedy, not a serious drama. He's got everyone on edge. We'll have a mutiny on our hands if he doesn't let up."

That mutiny suddenly seemed a reality. As Larry berated Catarina yet again for her overacting and high-pitched voice, aping the way she spoke in his falsetto, Cynthia stormed from the stage and came to where Melinda and I sat. She was on the verge of tears.

"I've had it, Melinda," she said. "Enough is enough."

"Calm down," Melinda said. "He'll get over it."

Larry's bellowing at Catarina continued from the stage.

"Tell him to leave her alone," Cynthia said, slumping into the chair next to me.

Melinda got up and went to the stage, where she engaged Larry in a private conversation off to the side.

"Nerves are frayed," I said.

"Tell me about it," Cynthia said.

"Paul's murder has everyone on edge," I said. "Has Detective Ladd spoken with you?"

She gave a rueful laugh and blew a strand of hair from her forehead. "Twice," she said. "You'd think he considers me a murderer. Or is it murderess?"

"I don't think it matters what we call it," I said. "Had you known Paul Brody before he joined the cast?"

She didn't answer.

"I'm only interested because—"

"The detective asked me the same question."

"I'm sure he did." I waited. "Did you?"

"Yes. In New York."

"How well did you know him?"

"Did I sleep with him? Is that what you're asking?"

"I'm only asking how well you knew him."

"Well, if you must know, Mrs. Fletcher, I didn't sleep with Paul."

I looked at the stage, where Catarina was now alone.

"I understand the young actress playing the maid had an affair with Paul in New York. Did you know that?"

"Sure. Everybody in the cast knows it." She turned to face me. "She didn't kill him," she said flatly, as though to think otherwise was demented.

"That's good to hear," I said. "Did Paul play any of his female roles when you knew him in New York?"

She looked at me as though *I* was demented. "Female roles? What female roles?"

"Maybe I'm mistaken," I said, "but the bio on his Web site says he did, in Los Angeles and San Francisco."

"Paul Brody play a woman? Oh, my God, what a joke. He always considered himself Mr. Macho, trying to bed every woman he met, young or old, fat or skinny, beautiful or plain."

"I wasn't suggesting he wasn't masculine. After all, many heterosexual male actors have successfully played females in movies and on the stage."

"Not Paul," she said.

"You seem certain that Catarina had nothing to do with his murder. Is there anyone else in the cast who might have had a motive to kill him?"

"He wasn't a well-liked person, Mrs. Fletcher. He crossed a lot of people. But would that be enough for someone to murder him? I can't imagine anyone going to that extreme."

"I can't either," I said, "but someone did—go to that extreme."

"Cynthia!" Larry called from the stage. "Come on. Let's do that scene again. We haven't got all day."

"Excuse me," Cynthia said, standing and straightening her clothing. "Simon Legree is calling."

I smiled as I watched her join Larry on the stage. He was obviously a demanding taskmaster, but despite how upset some cast members were, they seemed to respect him and tried to please.

The scene Larry ran through now involved only

Cynthia and Catarina. As I watched, Victoria took the seat next to me that Cynthia had vacated.

"Things going well?" I asked.

"Things are going terribly," she said. "I don't know what's gotten into Larry's head. He's wound tighter than a spring today."

"He's under a lot of pressure," I offered. "The play *and* the real murder."

"Paul's murder shouldn't concern him," she said.

"It concerns everyone," I said, a little taken aback at the callousness of her comment. "It's hard not to think about it, especially for you and the others on the stage. After all, that's where he died."

"I just want this to be over and to get out of here," she said. "I've had enough of Larry's hysterics and that detective's questions. He doesn't look to me like someone capable of solving anything."

As she said it, Detective Ladd entered the auditorium and took a seat directly behind us. Victoria turned, feigned a smile, and left. Ladd leaned on the back of her empty chair and said quietly, "I hear that the plows are on the job."

"That's good," I said, my tone reflecting the ambivalence I'd felt about the road being cleared.

"Anything new," he asked, "besides finding the murder weapon?"

"No. I wish I had something positive to offer."

"I wish you did, too. When will you be leaving?"

"Day after tomorrow. The official weekend ends tomorrow, but I decided to extend my stay by a day." I laughed. "I'd say I'm doing it to relax, but considering the circumstances, that doesn't make sense, does it?"

He touched my shoulder in a friendly gesture as he stood and stretched. "Going to the play tonight, Mrs. Fletcher?"

"Yes. Will you be there?"

"I suppose so. I've interviewed everyone in the hotel and came a cropper. See you later."

I watched the rehearsal to its conclusion. Larry and Melinda came to where I sat. "This show will be the death of me," Larry said, sprawling in a chair and rubbing his eyes. "Pardon the pun. I'm not sure continuing with the show was a good idea."

"Whether it was or not," I said, "that's the reality. I've been meaning to ask you all weekend about the redheaded woman."

"Oh? You mean that big gal who's got everyone in the hotel talking about her?"

"Yes. When does her role in the play become obvious?"

Larry and Melinda looked at each other with quizzical expressions. "She doesn't have a role with us," Larry said.

"She doesn't?"

Melinda laughed. "I can see why you would have thought she did," she said. "We always have a couple of ringers like that in our shows, but I decided that the cast for this show was big enough without adding anyone else. Why do you ask?"

"Just curious," I said. "I assumed all along she was with you."

"Sorry to disappoint," Larry said. "I'm glad she's not. I have enough trouble with the cast I have. I need a quick nap and a shower."

As he prepared to leave, Catarina walked past us and exited the auditorium. Larry waited until she was out of earshot before he mimicked her again, using his best female voice. "If I never hear her voice again, it will be too soon. See you at dinner."

"I'll go with you," Melinda said. "I could use ten minutes with my feet up, too. See you later, Jessica."

I decided to take a look outside to see how things were going with snow removal. I went to the main entrance and opened the door. There were no plows in sight, but I could hear the whine of their engines in the distance. I chatted for a minute with one of the officers on duty, then wandered down to Mohawk House's lower level and went to the door at which I'd first seen Paul Brody.

"Hello," I said to the officer there.

"Hi," he said, a smile crossing a face that sported a two-day beard. "I heard the plows are on their way."

"And I imagine that makes you very happy."

"Sure does," he said, "but it'll be a while before they clear things all the way up here. The mountain road is more than four miles long. You're Mrs. Fletcher, right? The writer."

"Yes, I am."

"Be here for a few minutes?"

"I suppose so."

"Mind if I disappear for a minute? Nature calling. No one should leave through this door."

"I'll hold the fort for you," I said.

He wandered away, leaving me alone just inside the door. Judging from a fresh supply of butts on the concrete floor, I concluded that some of the smokers in the crowd had found the spot. I thought back to that first meeting and replayed in my mind what had happened that night.

I'd been outside, gotten cold, and found this door. As I approached it, I heard a man and a woman arguing. When I opened the door, the woman— whoever she was—had already started up the stairs. But as I mulled this over, it struck me that the only reason I'd thought the second person was a woman was because of the second voice, distinctly female.

Or was it?

Larry Savoy's imitation of Catarina sounded female. I squeezed my eyes shut and tried to hear his voice again. If I hadn't known it was a man speaking in a falsetto, I would have assumed that I was hearing a woman. Was the female voice I heard from outside the door the same voice I'd just heard in the auditorium? I couldn't be sure, but it was a definite possibility.

The officer returned. "Thanks," he said. "Anybody show up?"

"No, just me," I said. "Glad you'll finally be able to leave and get some rest."

I walked up to the main floor, where I bumped into John Chasseur and his wife, Claudette. She wore a skintight white leotard and oversized sunglasses; Larry was in his usual T-shirt, serving as a billboard for his latest book, and jeans. Claudette returned my greeting but immediately walked away, saying she was on her way for a massage.

"Finger the killer yet, Jess?" Chasseur asked, grinning.

"Maybe," I said.

His eyes widened. "You sound serious."

"Oh, I am, very serious. By the way, I was wondering why neither you nor your wife mentioned that the actor who was killed had been in a movie you'd produced, and that Claudette appeared in."

His smiling face changed, less smug now. "Where did you hear that?" he asked.

"I did some checking. You obviously knew him before you came here to Mohawk House."

"I don't remember him. Probably had some walk-on part along with dozens of others."

"His bio says he played a character with a name and had a speaking role."

He shook his head and spoke to me as though I was the class dunce. "You believe what actors put on their bios, Jess, and you'll believe the moon is made of cheese. See ya."

I'm not a person who gloats over victories, but I couldn't help but smile in satisfaction at seeing the cocky, ego-driven John Chasseur a bit shaken.

Dinner promised to be interesting.

Chapter Twenty-two

*In the short story "Silver Blaze," the detective
solves the crime by observing that a dog failed
to act like a dog the night of the crime. Who
wrote it?*

Before going to my room to get ready for dinner, I
managed to speak with a few cast and crew members
I found wandering about the hotel. When I asked
whether they knew about the cross-dressing aspect
of Paul Brody's acting career, their reactions were uni-
formly incredulous, which posed a dilemma for me.
How had he managed to keep that phase of his professional life from everyone in the cast and crew? It
was there on his own Web site, along with photos
of him in women's clothing. Surely, someone must
have known.

Showered and dressed in a fresh outfit, I went to
the dining room, where my tablemates were already
seated. I was happy to see Claudette there with her
husband, the large sunglasses doing a good job of
shielding her bruises from the eyes of others. Judging
from the expression on her husband's face, he wasn't
especially pleased to see me. My comment to him
about Paul Brody having known him and Claudette

in Hollywood had obviously altered his mood. Gone was the wide, dazzling white smile and gregarious manner. He was downright sullen, and only muttered responses to comments and questions directed at him.

"Have a pleasant day, Jessica?" Boynton asked between sips of his martini.

"I don't know if I'd characterize it as pleasant, but it was productive. You?"

"Actually," the Englishman said, "I had a most interesting day. Didn't I, Georgie?"

She nodded. "Harold thinks he's solved the murder," she said.

"Oh, yeah?" Chasseur said. "The real one, or the one in the play?"

"The real one, sir," said Boynton proudly.

"Has your team made any progress?" I asked Chasseur.

"What team?"

"The one you formed with paying guests."

"The one that Jessica and ah thought was silly," Georgie chimed in, sounding pleased at having said it.

"I wasn't serious about it, but it sold books," Chasseur said.

Jody appeared to take our food orders. I noted that Chasseur didn't flirt with her, which pleased me. That sort of behavior in the presence of a spouse always makes me uncomfortable.

As we proceeded with our dinners, I took stock of others in the room. Most tables were occupied, some pushed together to accommodate members of various teams. Ms. Carlisle sat alone at a secluded table. The only time I'd ever seen anyone with her during meals was when Boynton had joined her at breakfast.

"So," I said to Boynton as Jody removed my salad plate and placed my entrée in front of me, "tell us who done it."

He seemed reluctant to respond, which prompted Georgie to answer for him. "Harold's only come to a speculative conclusion," she said, signaling to Jody that she wanted another Bacardi cocktail by pointing to her empty glass.

"Anybody can speculate," Chasseur said. "Big deal." He looked at me. "You say you may have solved it, Jessica, but I doubt whether you have anything more than speculation, too."

"You're probably right," I said.

"Tell us what you think," Claudette said to me, which surprised me. It was the first sign of interest she'd shown since we'd arrived at Mohawk House.

"I'd rather not," I said. "If any of us knows something that might shed light on the murder, Detective Ladd is the appropriate person to share it with."

"That country bumpkin?" Chasseur said, punctuating his words with a sardonic laugh. "You might as well tell our waitress, or the redhead over there." He nodded in Ms. Carlisle's direction. "Hey, Boynton, you seem chummy with her." He leaned toward Harold and asked, "What's she like under that black dress?"

Boynton ignored him, but I could see Chasseur's

arrogance was having its effect on the round Englishman. His face reddened, and a vein started pulsating in his neck.

"Ah have a good idea," Georgie said gleefully. "Why don't all of us here at this table write down who we think killed the actor? The winner gets some sorta prize."

"Like what?" Chasseur said. "Another weekend at this dump?"

Claudette spoke up again. "I would like to hear what Mrs. Fletcher has to say."

"What's so special about her?" her husband asked.

"Who do you think killed the actor?" she asked, lowering her sunglasses slightly on her nose and peering at me over them.

Before I had a chance to reply, she said, "Mrs. Fletcher obviously knows how to investigate a murder. She's done her homework and discovered that Paul Brody knew John and me in Hollywood."

"Shut up, Claudette," Chasseur said.

Claudette dismissed him and continued, "Paul and I were in a film together. John was one of a dozen so-called producers."

His face hardened.

"John also knows that Paul and I had an affair— a brief fling, really." She turned to her husband. "You did know that, didn't you, darling?"

"I told you to shut up," he said.

"That's no way to speak to a lady," Georgie Wick said, "especially one's wife. Go on, Mrs. Chasseur. Ah find this fascinating."

"Well, I don't," Chasseur said, throwing his napkin down on the table and stalking away.

"Why are you telling us this?" Boynton asked.

"Because it will come out anyway, thanks to Mrs. Fletcher," Claudette said. "John and I are now prime suspects. Isn't that right, Mrs. Fletcher?"

"It does focus some extra light on you," I said. "Did your affair with Paul Brody end badly?"

A sly smile crossed her pretty lips. "No, not at all. I wasn't angry with Paul—but John sure was."

An awkward silence descended on the table until I asked, "Did you know that Paul would be in the cast here this weekend?"

"Yes. John told me."

"And did you want to see him again?"

"No. John insisted I come, sort of a punishment. He's always looking for ways to punish me." She pushed back her chair, stood, leaned on the table, and said, "By the way, for all you sleuths, John wasn't in the audience when Paul was killed."

"Where was he?" Boynton asked.

"Probably out killing Paul," she said. "See you at the play."

Georgie broke the silence that accompanied Claudette's departure. "That is not a happy woman," she said.

"No surprise, married to an oaf like him," said Boynton. "Excuse me." He left the table and went to Ms. Carlisle, who had finished dinner and was drinking coffee. She extended her hand, which he kissed before taking a chair opposite her.

"Looks like Harold is smitten," I said.

"Harold is smitten by every woman he meets, Jessica. Pay him no mind. He's harmless and can be quite an entertaining traveling companion."

"If you say so."

"Ready to see the next act in the play?" she asked.

"I think so," I said. "But first, there's someone I must speak with."

"Who might that be?" she asked. At that moment Detective Ladd entered the dining room. Georgie saw him and said, "Oh, ah see. I'll bet you're about to solve the case for him."

"I had something like that in mind," I said. "Excuse me, Georgie. Save me a seat. I wouldn't want to miss a minute of it."

Chapter Twenty-three

Inspector Morse ranks among the most memorable characters created by British crime writers. Who introduced him to the reading public?

I spent twenty minutes with Detective Ladd before leaving the dining room and going to the auditorium.

Our conversation hadn't been particularly fruitful, although I did have a chance to present him with some of my conclusions. I told him what I'd learned about John and Claudette Chasseur's previous experience with Paul Brody, which he found especially interesting.

"Sounds to me," he'd said, "like you might have come up with the murderer."

It's possible that either Mr. or Mrs. Chasseur killed Brody," I said. "Motive is certainly present."

"The wife said her husband was probably out killing Brody?"

"Yes, that's what she said. But I considered it a flippant comment, not necessarily meaningful. What I can't unravel is this." I handed him the printout I'd made of Brody's Web site.

"What happened to the rest of it?" he asked. "Looks like it got cut off at the top."

"The hotel's printer needs adjusting, but not much is lost. Go ahead and read."

He flipped through the pages, pausing at each of the photographs and shaking his head. He handed them back to me with a sour expression on his thin, angular face, "Well, I'll be. The deceased dressed up in women's clothing, huh? I've heard about people like that and always wondered why they do it."

"Presumably because they like to," I said. "In Paul's case, it's how he made his living, at least part of the time. How long have you been with the police department?"

"Be fourteen years this coming September, but a detective just a short time. I have to admit I never ran across any men who dress up like women, but I suppose that's a big-city thing."

"Do you remember a theater called the Newsome?" I asked.

"Sure. Used to be what they call a legitimate theater. It's a movie house now. My wife and I used to go there to see traveling shows that came through, mostly musicals. My wife likes musicals. We saw some great ones, with real talented people."

"I'm sure you did. Do you happen to remember when Paul Brody was here one summer acting at the Newsome?"

"Can't say that I do."

"According to one of the hotel staff who's been here a long time, Brody spent a summer here acting at the theater and doing odd jobs around town to make ends meet."

"Doesn't ring any bells for me," he said.

"It was worth asking. Getting back to the bio and the fact that Mr. Brody spent a good part of his acting career appearing as a female impersonator, my problem is that no one who knew him seems to be aware of that aspect of his career."

"Well, maybe it's like him sneaking a smoke now and then. Doesn't want others to know."

"Perhaps," I said, "but I somehow think there's a lot more to it than that. I have a request."

"What's that, Mrs. Fletcher?"

"I'd appreciate it if you and some of your officers are present during the performance tonight."

He frowned.

"Is that a problem?" I asked.

"It's just that once the plows free up the road, I've got to let some of my men get home and grab some sleep."

"I understand," I said, "but I have a hunch that this evening's performance could wrap up your investigation."

The frown disappeared, replaced by eyebrows raised into question marks. "I'll be there," he said, "and I'll have a couple of my men with me."

"Thanks. That's all I can ask."

"Care to tell me more?"

"I'd love to, but I think it might be better to wait. Indulge me?"

He grinned. "I wouldn't think of doing anything else, Mrs. Fletcher."

Despite having spent the time with Detective Ladd, I was early for the performance and had my choice of seats. Mr. and Mrs. Pomerantz were already there, seated in the front row. As usual, they were dressed alike, this time wearing matching dark blue button-down shirts and light blue cardigans. On the opposite side of the room was Claudette Chasseur, minus her husband. A sheet of paper announcing the remaining schedule, and promoting various services offered by Mohawk House, was on each chair. I read mine before pulling from my pocket the printout of Paul Brody's Web site. *There has to be an answer to this*, I told myself, almost willing it to appear. This time, I read it from beginning to end, every line. It was on the last page that I found the answer. It was so simple, there in black and white had I taken the time to read all of the pages. What I was reading was not Paul Brody's Web site. It was the Web site of an actor named Peter Brody.

When I'd typed in Paul Brody's name on Google, the search engine had brought up anything that mentioned his name. In this case, the final page of Peter Brody's long bio contained the line: "He is the brother of another actor, Paul Brody."

I gasped. "They were twins. Identical twins."

No wonder I was confused. Seeing the pictures on the bio had reinforced for me the belief that I was reading Paul's résumé. I might have picked up on it earlier had the bio not constantly referred to Peter Brody as "Mr. Brody," and if the printer had not cut off the tops of the pages, including the headline on the first page.

My thoughts went back to when I'd seen a woman approach Paul Brody in the lobby, claiming to know him. If I remembered correctly, she'd called him Peter. That sort of mistaken identity must happen regularly with twins. There are myriad stories about how twins are constantly being confused for one another, even by those close to them. I'd even heard of instances in which a twin was able to fool his brother's girlfriend or wife.

Things began to fall into place for me now. Georgie Wick and Harold Boynton hadn't seen the ghost of Paul Brody on the third floor. They'd seen his twin brother, Peter. What other explanation could there be?

The man I'd seen smoking when I came in from my walk that first night was probably Peter, not Paul. Those who said Paul had quit smoking were right. Was it Peter who'd followed me on my sojourn through the inner recesses of the hotel? I couldn't be sure, but it was a reasonable assumption.

The auditorium was now filling up. Detective Ladd stood at the back of the room, two uniformed officers flanking him.

The big question!

Had Peter murdered his brother?

If so, it cast serious doubt on the theory I'd carried with me into the theater that night.

Larry Savoy bounded down the stairs at the side of the stage and headed for the rear of the auditorium.

"Larry," I said.

He stopped.

"Got a minute?"

"Not right now. Another crisis. Be back soon."

I was peering at the Web site printout, still dismayed at not having taken the time to read the entire document, resulting in my not picking up the difference in names, when Ms. Carlisle entered the auditorium, accompanied by Harold Boynton. I looked for Georgie Wick and spotted her sitting a few rows behind where Boynton and his tall, redheaded companion for the evening took seats in the front row. It was the first time I'd seen Ms. Carlisle at a performance. I couldn't imagine that Boynton would seriously be interested in her; it was a bizarre pairing of people if I ever saw one. But I learned years ago never to judge mutual attraction between men and women. Individuals see things in each other that outsiders don't, and it's silly to second-guess. Had I not known that she wasn't part of the cast, I would have anticipated her playing a role in the production at this performance.

Larry returned and plopped down beside me. "What's up?" he asked.

"Are you planning to have your detective call people up from the audience during this act?" Using audience members in the show was a staple theatrical device for Savoy productions. A number of preselected people would be called to the stage and asked humorous questions based upon information previously provided for the detective, hopefully generating funny responses. Most did, acting silly as the detective in the show used his quick wit and ad-lib ability to milk those situations for laughs.

"Sure. He's already got the list."

"Would you mind adding another to it?"

"You mean you're finally ready for your stage debut, Jessica?"

"No, not me," I said, smiling. "I have someone else in mind."

"Who would that be?"

"Ms. Carlisle."

He looked across the room to where she and Boynton sat. "Why her?" he asked.

"I think it might prove interesting. Will you do it?"

"Sure. I'll have Melinda come up with some material for Carboroni to use."

"No need to do that," I said, handing him a sheet on paper of which I'd written notes and questions for the detective.

Larry read what I'd written. "Will she go along with it?"

"I don't know, Larry, but it's worth a try."

"Does this have to do with Paul's murder?" he asked.

"Yes."

"Do you think that she—?"

"I'm not sure what I think at this moment," I said.

"I just know that we're running out of time. If the killer isn't apprehended right away, the weekend will be over and he or she will be gone forever."

"Okay," Larry said. "I'm with you, Jessica."

He returned to the stage, and I left my seat to join Detective Ladd.

"I wish you'd tell me more," he said.

"It won't be long," I said. "I figured out the problem with the Web site." I told him about the name mix-up.

"His twin is *here*?"

"I'd bet on it—if I were a betting person."

"Where is he? If he's been here all weekend and hiding out, he's number one on my suspect list."

"Along with a few others," I said. "Enjoy the show."

As I resumed my seat, I sensed that the audience was primed, ready to go. There was intense excitement throughout the auditorium. Did they know that something special was about to happen, or were they simply happy to see the weekend coming to an end and looking forward to leaving, now that they finally could? It didn't matter what was behind their enthusiasm. It was there, and I felt it the way professional entertainers must feel it every time they prepare to face an audience. Opera singers refer to stepping out on a stage in front of an audience as "facing the hungry wolf," and I have nothing but admiration for performers who are willing to expose themselves to a critical audience.

The theme from *The Pink Panther* came from the

speakers—the show was about to begin. Larry stepped through the curtains and was handed his wireless microphone by Melinda, who then went down into the audience to pass out the cards on which audience members would record their answers to the latest questions posed by Larry. One of them was mine, about the author who created the beloved Inspector Morse. There were groans from people who didn't know the answers, and satisfied exclamations from those who did.

"You've all been real troupers," Larry said as Melinda collected the cards. "Ready for the next installment in this story of murder, mayhem, and mysterious doings?" The audience responded appropriately. "But I must warn you before we begin. What you see tonight will curl your hair and push your pulse rates to new heights. It's not for the faint of heart!"

The curtain opened, and Detective Carboroni and Officer Dolt entered stage right, eliciting applause from the audience. Dolt stepped to the front of the stage and bowed dramatically, prompting Carboroni to elbow him aside and do the same. This time the audience booed. It was all great fun, and I was happy to see the audience enjoying it so much.

Carboroni began questioning the Whittakers while Catarina cowered off to the side. Cynthia assumed a defiant posture behind Carboroni, arms crossed across her chest, one foot tapping loudly on the stage floor. After a few minutes of baseless questioning, Carboroni turned to the audience, pulled a piece of paper from his trench coat, and read off a name. It was the

first of four names he would call over the next ten
minutes. One was the doctor who'd been brought
into things outside the dining room the first night.
Another was an extremely nervous woman who
could do nothing but giggle as Carboroni asked silly
questions about her life and career. She was, she told
him, a schoolteacher, which prompted Carboroni to
ask whether she thought she could teach Officer Dolt
anything. She said she doubted it, prompting Dolt
to announce that he'd graduated at the head of his
class in high school. Carboroni asked how many stu-
dents were in his graduating class. "Three," he said
proudly, obviously using a routine he and Carboroni employed whenever a teacher was rung into
the act.

Carboroni went through the four people, tying
them to the Whittaker family in absurd scenarios he
concocted. The audience loved it.

"All right, youse can sit down," Carboroni said,
"but don't leave." To Dolt, "Make sure they don't
leave the premisesses."

"It's premises," Dolt corrected.

Carboroni shot him an angry look, causing Dolt to
raise his hands in mock defense.

"Is there a Ms. Carlisle in the audience?" Carboroni asked.

Everyone turned to see whether the mysterious
redheaded woman dressed in black would respond
to his call.

"Come on, dear," Carboroni called. "You're the

most glamorous lady here. We couldn't miss a chance to talk with you."

She didn't move for a few seconds. But then she slowly stood, straightened her dress, and looked down at Boynton, who shook his head. She patted his bald pate, drew herself up to full height, and climbed the short set of steps, head high, carrying herself regally. She crossed the stage to where Carboroni stood, smiled at him, and waited for his question.

"Your name is Ms. Carlisle?" he asked.

"Yes."

"What's your first name?"

She replied coquettishly, "I only give my first name to men I know especially well."

"Yeah? Well, look, lady, I'm a police officer, and I don't take kindly to people who don't answer my questions."

"I like it when you're angry," she said, touching his cheek with the fingertips of her right hand, setting off a roar of laughter from the audience.

Carboroni jumped back in mock horror. "Don't touch me," he said. "I'm pledged to another."

"Don't touch the detective," Dolt said, walking in a circle around Ms. Carlisle and bending down to peer under her veil.

"You're cute," she said to Dolt. "I'd like to take you home with me as a mascot."

He beamed at the audience. More laughter.

Carboroni referred to the notes I'd provided. "I'm

here investigating a murder, Ms. Carlisle," he said, "and I have to know who my suspects are. Sorry, but the veil has to go."

She gasped in shock at what he'd suggested.

"Come on, Ms. Carlisle," he said, "don't play games with an officer of the law—which is what I happen to be."

"If you insist," she said.

Instead of following his order where she stood, she sauntered to the front of the stage and looked down at the audience, batting her long eyelashes and thrusting out one hip. "I have the feeling I am about to be exposed," she said, laughing softly. Then, in one swift, unexpected motion, she whipped off her black veil and red wig and tossed them into the crowd.

"I am," she said in a dramatic female voice, "Paul Brody."

There were gasps, followed by loud expressions of disbelief by some, affirmation by others.

"I knew he wasn't dead," a man yelled as Ms. Carlisle continued to disrobe until she'd shucked her long black dress and women's shoes and stood there in a pair of running shorts and a T-shirt.

My attention went to Harold Boynton, who looked as though he'd gone into permanent shock. He leaned forward in his seat, mouth hanging open, confusion written all over him as he stared at the "woman" who'd been his seat companion only moments earlier.

Detective Ladd came up the aisle, flanked by the

two uniformed officers. He looked up at Brody, who'd assumed a dramatic pose, a broad smile on his heavily made-up face. "Arrest him," Ladd said.

I stepped up next to the detective and said, "No, not yet."

"This isn't in the script," Monroe Whittaker intoned from the stage.

Larry Savoy came from the wings and asked me, "What's this all about, Jessica?"

"It's about the murder of Paul Brody," I said.

"He wasn't murdered," a woman in the audience said. "See? They did it to throw us off."

I waited for the conversations to cease. "I'm afraid you're wrong," I said to the woman. "Paul was murdered, both in the play and in reality. This isn't Paul Brody. This is his twin brother, Peter."

"He looks just like Paul," a man exclaimed.

"Identical twins usually do," I said.

I climbed the steps to the stage and stood next to Peter, who was going through a series of poses for the audience, the smile never leaving his face. "Why did you come here?" I asked. Carboroni brought the microphone to us so the audience could hear.

"Why, to kill my brother, of course," he responded, sounding gleeful.

Detective Ladd started up the stairs, but I shook my head and held up my hand. I said to Peter, "Why did you want to kill Paul?"

"To get even," he said, no longer using his forced feminine voice. He was now a baritone. "He had all the breaks in life, thanks to daddy dearest, and he even stole what money was left to me. My brother was not a very nice person. I hated him."

Behind us, Victoria Whittaker said to Melinda, "This is better than the script."

In front of us, someone shouted, "Help!" I looked to where Harold Boynton had apparently fainted, pitching forward off his seat to the floor. Those close to him fell to their knees, and the physician who'd been on the stage joined them and took over reviving him, with Georgie Wick at his side.

"Oh, poor Harold," Peter said. "I'm afraid the shock was too much for him. Such a dear man."

This time, Detective Ladd and the two officers wouldn't be put off. They mounted the stage, and Ladd confronted Peter. Carboroni held the microphone in front of him as the detective said, "You're under arrest for the murder of Paul Brody."

"I don't think so," I said.

"He confessed," Ladd said. "He said he came here to kill his brother." To Peter: "Isn't that right, young—man?"

I answered for him. "He said he came here with that intention, Detective, but he didn't say he went through with his plan."

Ladd faced Peter again. "Well, did you kill your brother?"

"I would have," Peter said, "but someone beat me to it."

"Who?" Ladd asked me.

I looked out over the audience and saw that John Chasseur, who'd joined his wife, had gotten up and was heading for the door. "I don't think anyone should be allowed to leave," I said to Ladd.

"Hey," Ladd shouted. "Mr. Chasseur. You can't leave."

Chasseur stopped just short of the door. "I'll go wherever and whenever I want," he said.

"No sir, you will not," Ladd replied, sounding as though he meant it. He instructed the two uniformed officers to go to the door and prohibit anyone from leaving the auditorium. Chasseur muttered under his breath as one of the officers escorted him to his seat next to Claudette.

I took the microphone from Carboroni and addressed the audience. "You've all had a chance to meet John Chasseur and his lovely wife, Claudette. You may know that John is a successful writer and Claudette was a Hollywood actress. What you may not have known is that they knew Paul Brody in Hollywood. He was in a film that John produced, and in which Claudette appeared."

A wave of murmurs rolled across the auditorium. Many people pulled out their pads and began scribbling.

"So what?" Chasseur called from where he sat. "What does that prove?"

"It doesn't prove anything on the surface," I said, "but you both know that certain things happened in Hollywood with Paul that provide you, John, with a motive for wanting him dead."

Chasseur stood. "That may be," he said, "but wanting somebody dead isn't against the law."

"That's true," I said, "but battering one's wife is."

He looked down at Claudette and muttered an obscenity.

I returned my attention to Peter Brody. "Why did you stay?" I asked. "Once you knew that your brother was dead, why didn't you leave?"

"Oh, I don't know," he replied. "I thought about leaving, but the snowstorm changed my mind. Besides, I was having too much fun." He looked to where Harold Boynton had come to and was back in his seat. Georgie Wick sat next to him in the chair that Peter Brody, aka Ms. Carlisle, had occupied. "I'm glad you're feeling better, Harold," Peter said. "I apologize for misleading you."

"You stayed because you were having fun making people think you were a woman?" I said.

"Yes. Why not? After all, I make my living doing that." He told the audience: "If you're ever in San Francisco, you must come and see the show I'm in." He mentioned the name of the nightclub a few times, then turned to me and asked, "Anything else, Mrs. Fletcher? Am I free to go?"

"You followed me when I explored some out-of-the-way places in the hotel, didn't you?"

He nodded.

"Why?"

"Why not? My friend Harold told me that you would probably solve the murder of my brother, so I thought I'd see what you were up to. By the way, have you solved his murder? Not that I care very much."

"That remains to be seen," I said. "Mind another question?"

"Ask all you want."

"You and your family used to come here to Mohawk House when you and Paul were little."

"Yeah. I loved this place. We were constantly exploring to find the secret rooms and passages, playing pranks on the staff. I wished we could live here."

"You did for a while," I said, "as an adult. You came back here one summer to appear in summer stock at a theater, the Newsome."

His brow furrowed. "That's right," he said, drawing out the words as if he had trouble remembering.

"And you did odd jobs in order to make ends meet."

He forced a laugh. "You've really been digging, haven't you?"

"I'm a good listener," I said. "People at this hotel thought it was Paul who'd come here that summer. But when Paul was reminded of it, he said he had no memory of it. That's because it was you, not Paul."

He laughed again. "I've pretended to be Paul many times, Mrs. Fletcher. That's one of the few advantages of being an identical twin. There aren't many advantages, especially when your father favors one over the other. The old man always preferred Paul to me, gave him financial backing when Paul was trying to break into Hollywood. He never did that for me. I have a lot more acting talent than Paul ever did, but he got all the breaks. A lot of good it did him, huh? He's dead and I'm very much alive."

I noticed that members of the audience were frantically taking notes. Did they still think this was part of the play? Obviously, some did. The cast onstage stood mute, taking it all in.

"Okay, Mrs. Fletcher," Detective Ladd said, "this has all been very interesting. But if this Mr. Brody—Paul. No, Peter—whatever—if he isn't a murderer, who is?"

"I wouldn't say Peter Brody isn't a murderer," I said.

"But I thought you said that—"

I walked to the side of the stage near where Mr. and Mrs. Pomerantz were seated. He sat stone-still, his eyes glazed, looking straight ahead.

"Mr. Pomerantz," I said.

He slowly raised his head to look at me. His expression hadn't changed. He had the look of someone who'd just had a devastating message delivered to him.

"Quite a shock, isn't it, Mr. Pomerantz?" I said.

He sat in silence.

"You thought it was Paul Brody who'd strangled your wife, didn't you?"

"I killed the wrong man," he said so softly I almost missed it.

I turned to Peter Brody. "If Mr. Pomerantz wanted to avenge his wife's murder, he should have focused on you. You'd spent the summer in this area pretending to be your brother, Paul."

"He was off in Hollywood making dirty movies. He never knew I pretended to be him," he said. A faraway look came into his eyes. "It was the only time my father ever gave me a pat on the back— when he thought I was Paul."

"What happened with Mrs. Powell?" I asked.

He squirmed. "She caught me stealing money and said she was going to call the police."

"So you strangled her?"

He seemed to realize all of a sudden that he was still onstage. "I didn't say that," he said. "You didn't hear me say that. I want a lawyer."

Mr. Pomerantz was now on his feet and approaching the stage, his wife close behind him. They climbed the steps and came directly to where Peter Brody stood with Detective Ladd. Carboroni, the detective in the play, continued to hold the microphone, moving it from speaker to speaker like a talk show host interviewing guests.

"All these years," Pomerantz said, "I've been accused of having murdered my wife. I've had to live with it and turn my back on the cruel comments people made about me and Ethel"— he pointed to his new wife—"I had to turn the other cheek, excuse them for their behavior. I've spent the years since the murder trying to find her killer, using every cent I made to pursue justice. I finally narrowed it down to only one person—Brody, who was here that summer acting in a play and doing odd jobs. My wife told me she'd hired someone to help do some gardening and other small jobs around the house, but she never told me his name. He'd only worked at the house for two days, and just a few hours at that. And then he killed her. I've devoted my life to finding him, and I thought I had."

He fixed Peter Brody in a hard stare. "But I was wrong. It was you."

It occurred to me as I listened to his confession that he no longer spoke with the catch in his throat. Had this moment of soul-cleansing rid him of that affliction? His wife, who'd stood stoically by his side, her hand in his, said in a quiet voice, "It's all right, Sydney. You did what you felt you had to do. Everything will be all right."

One of the uniformed officers led Pomerantz away.

Ladd said to Peter Brody, "Looks like we got two murders solved at once. You're under arrest, too, for the murder of Mrs. Sydney Powell."

"Don't be ridiculous," Brody said.

"Take him away," Ladd instructed the other officer.

Brody put up a struggle but was no match for the brawny officer and Ladd.

Up until the arrest, the audience had watched and listened in rapt attention. Now a cacophony of voices broke out, everyone eager to discuss the scene they'd witnessed. I looked at Larry Savoy, whose expression was bewildered.

"What do we do next?" he said.

I leaned over the microphone still held by Carboroni, "There's one more murder to be solved," I said. "The one in the play."

I turned to Larry and the cast. "I think your audience is anxious to see if they've correctly solved the mystery."

"You mean—?"

"Yes! The show must go on."

Chapter Twenty-four

Who wrote the 1868 mystery **The Moonstone?**

As was so often the case with the Savoys' interactive murder mystery weekends, it was virtually impossible to come up with the solution on the basis of what was presented onstage. This play was no exception. In Melinda's convoluted script, Victoria, the mother, had had an affair with Paul's father, the New York City cop, and had given birth to a son she put up for adoption. She shot Paul, her own son, to keep Cynthia—the daughter she and Monroe had together—from marrying the young man, and in the process committing incest. And Paul was actually an undercover cop looking to get the goods on Monroe, an embezzler, using Cynthia to get close to him and trying to keep the maid, his former lover, from exposing who he really was.

There were many moans the next day when, after each team had presented their conclusions, this plot was revealed by Larry and Melinda. The winning team was nowhere close to having figured out the murder mystery, but they put on a delightfully creative sketch that wowed the judges, including myself. An older man got the most correct answers to the questions posed by Larry, and won a free weekend at Mohawk House. But while the performances had been fun, the real murder of Paul Brody dominated most conversations. The morning ended with a round of applause for the winners and for all the participants.

The road had been cleared, allowing the guests to leave and the local reporter, Todd Waisbren, and a few other media types to arrive and seek out anyone willing to make statements about what had happened over the weekend. John Chasseur was among those interviewed. "I knew all along who murdered Paul Brody," I heard him say. He spoke at length, giving his opinions on what had transpired as if he alone had the key to the case.

I smiled and slipped away before an enterprising reporter could waylay me. I was determined to use my final hours at the hotel to relax and to put what had occurred behind me, to think of anything and everything but murder.

But I couldn't avoid discussing it in the dining room when I sat down to lunch with Larry and Melinda Savoy, Georgie Wick, Harold Boynton, and Mark Egmon.

"Okay, Jessica," Mark said, "we're all waiting to hear how you knew it was Mr. Pomerantz who killed Brody."

"I couldn't be sure," I said, "but I was pretty confident after a conversation I had with him. He suggested that a kitchen worker might be the murderer because he'd have easy access to knives and cleavers. As far as I knew, I was the only hotel guest who was privy to the fact that Brody had been stabbed, not shot."

"How did you know that?" Melinda asked.

"Detective Ladd had taken me into his confidence. I knew he'd never have given the same information to Mr. Pomerantz, since he suspected him of murdering his first wife. So, I concluded that if Mr. Pomerantz knew the victim had been stabbed, it could only be because he was the killer."

"Speaking of the detective, Jessica, how did he take it that it was you who identified the murderer, and not he?"

"I don't think it disturbed him at all. He's a nice man, not at all competitive. He was really pleased that, along with the Brody killing, the murder of Mr. Pomerantz's wife also got solved. That file had been inactive for years, but he maintained an ongoing interest in it. Of course, the police may have a difficult time proving to a jury that Peter Brody killed Mrs. Pomerantz—I mean Mrs. Powell. That was Pomerantz's former name. Detective Ladd called me to say that the story appeared in the local paper this morning, including Peter Brody's picture. He's hoping it will cause someone with damaging evidence against Brody to come forward. Only time will tell whether he's convicted or not. Detective Ladd promised to stay in touch and keep me informed."

"I feel very sorry for Mr. Pomerantz," Georgie

Wick said. "Poor man. He was innocent of killing his wife, but now he's guilty of murder. If he found out it was Brody—that's Peter, not Paul—who killed his wife, why didn't he just go to the police and clear his name?"

"Detective Ladd asked him that same question, Georgie, and his answer was that he was afraid there wasn't enough hard evidence to convict Brody of his wife's murder. Of course, he thought it was Paul Brody, not Peter, and he was wrong. Paul was innocent of murdering anyone but paid the ultimate price."

Boynton hadn't said a word during the discussion. He avoided eye contact and focused on his food, and his martinis. I knew he was feeling acute embarrassment. I decided to try and ease his discomfort.

"It's remarkable," I said, "how effective Peter Brody was in portraying himself as a woman. I never doubted for a moment that he was just that, a woman—until toward the very end when I learned some things that led me to a different conclusion."

Boynton looked up at me and managed a small smile. "Thank you, Mrs. Fletcher," he said. "This old fool needs some understanding."

"Oh, Harold," Georgie said, placing her hand on his arm, "you're not an old fool. You're just—well, you're just a romantic at heart. Isn't he, Jessica?"

I nodded and smiled. "We need more romantics in the world," I said, not adding that I would prefer that they keep their hands to themselves.

We had dessert and coffee and prepared to say good-bye.

"You're staying until tomorrow?" Georgie asked me.

"That was my original plan, but I've changed my mind. I think I'll relax a lot more at my home in Cabot Cove. I have a driver picking me up in a half hour."

"Ah know one thing," Georgie said as we said farewell. "At least y'all know I wasn't seeing things when I said I saw the actor after he was killed. 'Course, it wasn't him. I'm kinda disappointed it wasn't his spirit. I thought it was my first real contact with the other world. It's something I've been dreaming about."

"And writing about," Harold added.

"Yes, for a long time. But this wasn't my imagination. I did see something."

"You certainly did," I agreed. "But before we go our separate ways, there's still a mystery to be solved here at Mohawk House."

"What's that?" Mark Egmon asked.

"What do your initials, *GSB*, stand for, Georgie?"

A small smile crossed her small, delicate face. She downed what was left of her Bacardi cocktail, smacked her lips, and said, "Ah'm afraid even the great Jessica Fletcher won't be solving that mystery. Come, Harold, it's time we left."

Detective Ladd called me at home four months later to tell me that a grand jury had indicted Peter Brody for the murder of Mrs. Powell. After a second person came forward, Brody confessed, and a plea bargain was struck that would keep him in prison for a minimum of sixty years. Sydney Pomerantz's lawyer built a case for insanity, and Pomerantz was committed to a state institution. I couldn't help but wonder whether his wife would visit on a regular basis and bring him clothing to match what she wore each time. And I wondered whether John and Claudette Chasseur were still married. If they were, I just hoped she'd learned some self-defense.

I did a lot of thinking about my weekend at Mohawk House and the events that had turned a good-natured theatrical murder into a real one. I'd been right about Sydney Pomerantz having stabbed Paul Brody to death, but there were other questions that I'd never been able to resolve to my satisfaction, the cigarette butts on my room's balcony being one of them. Since Paul Brody didn't smoke, it must have been his twin brother who'd gone out there to indulge his habit, perhaps to pique Paul's curiosity as mine had been piqued. Peter seemed to enjoy that sort of mischief.

Melinda Savoy also called to ask whether I would participate in another interactive murder mystery weekend they'd booked.

"I don't think so," I said. "I'm contenting myself these days with writing about murder, Melinda, not experiencing it firsthand. But thanks for thinking of me."

It was good to be home.

Answers to the questions posed at Mohawk House's Murder Mystery Weekend, which appear at the beginning of each chapter.

Chapter 2   In what Agatha Christie book did her Belgian detective, Hercule Poirot, make his first appearance?
ANS: *The Mysterious Affair at Styles* (1920)

Chapter 3   Which mystery writer features cats and dogs in her novels?
ANS: Lilian Jackson Braun

Chapter 4   The origin of the detective story is generally attributed to what nineteenth-century writer?
ANS: Edgar Allan Poe

Chapter 5   The characters Nero Wolfe and Archie Goodwin resided in a brownstone on West Thirty-fifth Street in Manhattan. Who created them?
ANS: Rex Stout

Chapter 6   Who wrote the hard-boiled detective novel, *I, the Jury*?
ANS: Mickey Spillane

Chapter 7   What British mystery writer also writes psychological crime novels under the pseudonym Barbara Vine?
ANS: Ruth Rendell

Chapter 8   *The Postman Always Rings Twice* was published in 1934. Who wrote it?
ANS: James M. Cain

Chapter 9   John Dickson Carr specialized in a certain type of murder mystery plot. What was it?
ANS: The locked-room mystery

Chapter 10   The first Shamus Awards were presented at Bouchercon in San Francisco in 1982. What genre of crime writing do the awards honor?
ANS: Private eyes

Chapter 11   A certain era is considered to be the "Golden Age" of murder mysteries. Was it the 1920s through the 1940s? The 1950s until the late 1970s? Or the 1980s through the mid-1990s?
ANS: 1920s through the 1940s

Chapter 12   Clint Eastwood starred in the film version of *Firefox*, penned by a leading British thriller writer. Who is he?
ANS: Craig Thomas

Chapter 13   In what book did Dame Agatha Christie introduce her enduring character Miss Marple?

ANS: *Murder at the Vicarage* (1930)

Chapter 14   What writer wrote nine books that featured sustaining characters Grave Digger Jones and Coffin Ed Johnson?

ANS: Chester Hines

Chapter 15   The daughter of a former U.S. president has written more than twenty murder mysteries set in Washington, D.C. Who is she?

ANS: Margaret Truman

Chapter 16   Many actors have played Agatha Christie's famed detective, Hercule Poirot, in movies. Name three.

ANS: Albert Finney, Peter Ustinov, Tony Randall, Austin Trevor, David Suchet

Chapter 17   Many writers of murder mysteries focus on a specific city or region. What places did (or do) the following writers regularly use as settings for their books? Lawrence Block, Raymond Chandler, Tony Hillerman, and Ralph McInerny.

ANS: New York City, Los Angeles, the Southwest, Indiana

Chapter 18   What writer created the Dortmunder gang in a series of comic crime novels?

ANS: Donald Westlake

Chapter 19   Some mystery writers make good use of history in their novels. One introduced readers to a medieval monk, Brother Cadfael, who dabbled in solving crimes. Name this author.

ANS: Ellis Peters

Chapter 20   What was Ed McBain's real name?

ANS: Evan Hunter

Chapter 21   The popular TV show *Diagnosis Murder*, which starred Dick Van Dyke, has been resurrected in a series of original novels. Who writes them? (Hint: He used to be the TV show's executive producer and writer.)

ANS: Lee Goldberg

Chapter 22   In the short story, "Silver Blaze," the detective solves the crime by observing that a dog failed to act like a dog the night of the crime. Who wrote it?

ANS: Sir Arthur Conan Doyle

Chapter 23   Inspector Morse ranks among the most memorable characters created by British crime writers. Who introduced him to the reading public?

ANS: Colin Dexter

Chapter 24   Who wrote the 1868 mystery *The Moonstone*?

ANS: Wilkie Collins

Read on for a sneak peak at the next exciting *Murder, She Wrote* original mystery, *Three Strikes and You're Dead* Coming from New American Library in October 2006

"We're down to the Rattlers' last out, folks, and the tension is palpable in Thompson Stadium—bottom of the ninth, the score three-two, with the Texans on top, two outs and the tying run on base. If the Rattlers fail to pull it out here, it will be back to the showers and another year before they get a chance to win a league championship and bask in the glory."

"Shortstop Junior Bennett, number fourteen, is up next, Ralph, but he's oh-and-three for the day against this left-handed pitcher. Think they'll leave him in?"

The camera focused on a heavily perspiring young fan wearing a number-14 Rattlers jersey over a Hawaiian shirt. He held up a sign that read JUNIOR FOR MVP. Ralph Trienza checked the TV monitor before lifting his red-and-green ball cap to wipe his brow with a handkerchief. "Wishful thinking on the part of that young man, don't you think, Doug?" he said, as the camera swung back to the two announcers. "Junior's been in a slump for a month, and Washington's been trying to let him play through it. But there's a lot at stake today. If I was a betting man—and I am—I'd have to go with a right-handed pinch-hitter here."

"I'm with you, Ralph. Washington has Ty Ramos on the bench. Ramos has had a good year. He's batting three-ten, three-twenty-five against left-handers. That's a pretty convincing argument."

"Might not be enough to satisfy H.B., though. Ty's got that strained hamstring that kept him from starting today. But Washington said in the pregame that Ty's available for pinch-hitting." Trienza looked into the camera. "You're watching KRM-TV, and I'm Ralph Trienza, with Doug Worzall, coming to you from Thompson Stadium in Mesa, Arizona, with the score three-two and a lot of folks wondering what manager Buddy Washington will decide to do. We'll find out in a minute, but first a few words from our sponsor."

"Who's H.B.?" I asked my friend Meg Duffy as the bright light trained on the announcers was switched off, and the monitor reflected a commercial for Thompson Tools and Hardware. With our seats next to the broadcast booth behind the visiting team's dugout, we could watch the game and listen to the local station's play-by-play at the same time.

The organist struck up "Take Me Out to the Ball Game," and a dozen cheerleaders ran out onto the field, behind the first-base foul line. They performed an acrobatic dance routine that ended with each cheerleader holding up a letter on a card, which together spelled out THOMPSON TOOLS. A boy on the end held both the *L* and the *S*.

I was in Arizona visiting an old school friend, Meg Hart Duffy, and her husband, Jack—Judge Jack Duffy to his legions of fans *and* detractors in the Family Division of the Superior Court, Hudson County, in the state of New Jersey—who had invited me to join them in Mesa, where they'd rented a house for the baseball season. The Rattlers were a Double-A team in the Pacific West division, and we were rooting for them to win. But even more, we were rooting for Ty Ramos to get to play in what was the final day of the season for the Rattlers. Ty was the Duffys' foster son.

"H.B. is Harrison Bennett, Senior, the team's owner," Meg said in answer to my question.

"Is he related to the shortstop?"

She nodded, and her eyebrows flew up. "Junior is his son. And you can see why it's been hard for Ty to get time on the field when they both play the same position. Buddy Washington tries his best—he knows Ty's the better player—but the orders come from above, and Junior gets preference. It's been very frustrating."

"I imagine it would be."

"Jack won't come to watch the game if Junior's playing. He even did some research to see if Bennett's actions were a breach of league rules, but there's no regulation about an owner's conduct if he has a son on the team. It may be unethical, and certainly not good for the team, but it isn't illegal. Too bad for us."

It was late afternoon. The Arizona sky was a clear blue, the sun still high enough to heat the stadium to a constant simmer. Summer in my home of Cabot Cove, Maine, is plenty hot, but it never reaches the thermometer heights of the Arizona desert.

"Couldn't Ty play another position?" I asked, fanning myself with the program.

"The manager uses him in the outfield every now and then to keep his bat in the lineup, but the regular outfielders complain when they have to sit one out. No one wants to miss a chance to play. Besides, Ty likes the action at shortstop. It's a busy position, and he thrives when there's lots to do."

"I guess he'll have to learn to be patient then."

"Not for long. At least I hope not." Meg lowered her voice and leaned closer to me. "We heard there was a scout from New York down here last week talking to the manager about Ty."

"So he has a good chance to move up to the major leagues?"

"Most likely Triple-A first. The Rattlers are in the Chicago Cubs' farm system. They have a good Triple-A team here in Arizona, too. Of course, there's always the possibility of a trade to another major-league ball club. It doesn't matter who he ends up playing for as long as he makes it to 'the Show.' That's what the kids call the majors, 'the Show.' That's what we're all praying for. Everyone tells us how talented he is. All he needs is a little more experience. He'd get it on a Triple-A team once he's out from under Junior and Harrison Bennett. If he does, it could be less than a year before he gets called up."

"Does he have a say on who he wants to play for?"

"He'd be happy with any team, I'm sure. He loves the Cubs and their history." She laughed. "Everything except their inability to get to the World Series. Naturally, his heart's set on playing in New York, for the Mets or even the Yankees." Meg shivered despite the heat. "To be candid, I kind of hope he'll get to see another part of the country, San Francisco or Tampa or St. Louis, rather than New York."

"But wouldn't playing for a New York team bring him closer to your home in New Jersey? You're only across the river from the city."

"True, and we do love to attend his games. But New York is a big city, with big-city temptations, and it's too close to Jersey City, where he had all that trouble when he was younger. I'd like to see him stay away from those kind of influences. He's still so young and impressionable."

Ty Ramos was only eleven years old the first time he was brought up before Judge Duffy on a charge of juvenile delinquency. His mother, who lived in the Dominican Republic, had sent Ty to live with an uncle in New Jersey, hoping to give her only son the benefits and opportunities of a life in the U.S. Instead, the uncle, who worked two jobs to support his own children, had little time to watch over yet another youngster. Ty was left to fend for himself inside a school where he didn't speak English and where teachers were overwhelmed by a student body with myriad problems. Outside on the streets was no better. The young boy learned to endure beatings by the older bullies, most of them gang members, who demanded his jacket and gloves in the winter, his baseball cap in the summer. He hid his lunch money in his shoes until they took those from him as well.

Homesick and angry, he was a magnet for trouble, fighting in school, straying out all night, stealing change from his uncle's pockets and fruit from the corner grocery. He joined the gang that had tormented him, carried a knife in his boot, and earned money by warning the drug dealers when a police car turned the corner and delivering messages for the owner of a local bar-owner, a low-level mobster who liked the fact that his errand boy didn't understand enough English to testify against him. That hadn't really been true anymore, but Ty let him believe it was.

Judge Duffy watched as an innocent first-time offender began to harden into a career criminal, and felt he had to intervene. Ty's situation reminded the judge of his own childhood in a poor neighborhood in Trenton, where he had to fight hard for respect and even harder to finish his education. Sending Ty back to the Dominican Republic was not an option. His mother had moved, and no one could locate her. Sending him back to his uncle would only perpetuate the problems. Foster family after foster family rejected the boy as too disruptive to keep. But Judge Duffy saw a spark in Ty that the others had missed.

He recognized a yearning to fit in, beneath the shield of resentment the teenager wore like armor, and Jack Duffy thought he might be able to reach Ty Ramos.

The first couple of years with Ty at the Duffys' sprawling suburban ranch were daunting. More than once Meg thought Jack had taken on more than they could handle, but through a combination of love and discipline, they began to see a change. Ty's transformation was helped by a new high school away from his old friends and enemies, one with strong academics and an even stronger sports program. Ty blossomed once he joined the baseball team, first as a catcher—the only boy willing to catch the streaking fastball of the team's star pitcher—and later as a first baseman. But he was to shine brightest at shortstop, the perfect position for his quick moves and accurate ability to read the batter.

There was no question of college when Ty graduated from high school, although not due to lack of achievement. He wasn't an honors student, but he'd acquitted himself well academically, passing all his tests with respectable grades, even the English literature exam, on which he'd scored an 89. But Ty had found his home in baseball, and an offer from the Cubs to join its Rattlers farm team had sealed his future—at least the immediate future.

"We're back, and Buddy Washington is in the dugout talking to his shortstops."

Ralph Trienza peered into the monitor as the camera trained its lens on the manager seated in the dugout. "Okay," Trienza said, "he's given the signal. Ty Ramos will pinch-hit for Junior Bennett."

A round of cheers greeted Ty as he climbed up the stairs from the dugout, picked up two bats and swung them over his shoulder, choosing one and dropping the other before taking his place at home plate.

"There's no love lost between those two," Doug Worzall said into his microphone. "Ramos and Bennett have been battling it out all season for a permanent slot at shortstop. They're not exactly friendly competitors, according to people close to the situation. That was a tough call to yank Junior."

"But a good one for the team, Doug. It's hard going up against Evans, a left-handed pitcher. Now we'll see if Ramos can pull it off. A hit here would put the winning run on base and bring up Carter Menzies, who's three for three today. But if Ramos fans, it's the end of the season for the Rattlers. Tough position to be in. There's a lot riding on those shoulders."

A chorus of boos swelled up from the vicinity of the left field fence. Meg took my hand and squeezed it.

"Those boo-birds out there are from San Pedro," Doug Worzall announced as the camera panned a contingent of Texan fans wearing yellow and red shirts, the team colors, and waving "We're Number One" foam hands.

"Here's the first pitch. It's a swing and a miss. That ball was outside, out of the strike zone. Looks like Ramos might be a little anxious."

"That corner is the pitcher's favorite, Ralph. Evans has left a lot of Rattlers swinging at that curveball."

"C'mon, Ty," Meg whispered, watching her foster son intently. "You can do it."

"Here's the windup. It's outside. One-and-one."

Ty used his bat to knock dirt from between his cleats, and twisted his right foot into the batter's box. He nodded to the umpire and squinted at the pitcher, taking a practice swing.

"Ramos is an interesting guy, Doug. He was born in the Dominican Republic. That country has baseball in its blood. It's the national passion. They've contributed more ballplayers to Major League Baseball than any other nation outside our borders, and with a population of less than nine million. Amazing, isn't it?"

The next pitch was low and outside, a ball.

"Those population numbers are almost the same as New Jersey's," Trienza said. "And don't forget that's where Ramos was raised. He was an all-star on his high school team, took them to the state championships."

"He's looking to take the Rattlers to the league championships now. Here's the pitch. Ooh, he fouled that one off his instep. Got to sting. Two-and-two."

The pitcher took off his mitt and rubbed the ball between his hands, pinching the top with his fingers as if he wanted to smooth out the leather. He stretched his back, put the glove back on, leaned over, and stared at the catcher, shook his head, then nodded and threw the ball. Ty jumped back as the ball whizzed by close to his head. He stepped out of the batter's box and swung his bat twice.

"That was a close one, Doug. Evans was giving him a warning there—don't crowd the plate. It's a full count, folks, in the bottom of the ninth with two out. This next pitch could decide the game."

Worzall laughed. "I'm feeling nervous myself, Ralph," he said. "Imagine what Ramos must be feeling now. The whole team is counting on him. That's a lot of pressure for a young player."

"But he's poised, Doug. Mature for his age. Let's see what he does with this pitch."

Ty tapped home plate with his bat, tugged on the peak of his cap underneath the batting helmet, and stole a glance at Meg. A small smile played around his lips. He adjusted his hips, swaying from side to side, lifted one shoulder after the other, then settled down into his batting crouch and waited. The pitcher wiped his lips, set the ball at his waist, reared back, raised his right leg and hurled the ball toward home plate.

Ty swung. There was a loud crack as his bat connected with the ninety-mile-an-hour fastball. The crowd rose to their feet, and Meg and I joined them to watch the ball sail toward the right field wall. The Texan outfielder skipped backwards, keeping his eye on the ball, then turned to watch it clear the fence and bounce on the street outside the stadium.

"Home run! The ball game's over. Ty Ramos hits a homer to end the game. The Rattlers have won the championship, with Ramos' long ball bringing in two runs for a four-three victory over the San Pedro Texans. Here come the tying and winning runs down the third-base line. The San Pedro Texans will have to wait another year. The Mesa Rattlers are the Pacific West Double-A champions!"

Meg gave me a hug, the tears streaming down her cheeks. "Oh, Jessica. He did it. He won the game. I'm so excited. I'm so proud. I knew he could do it."

"Congratulations, Meg. What a wonderful day for you and Jack."

"Oh, I know Jack saw this. He's watching our boy on TV."

Around us, fans were jumping up and down, screaming and laughing, giving each other high-fives. The cheerleaders bounced onto the grass, doing back flips and somersaults. The team mascot, an oversized character in a carpenter costume, wiggled his hips and pumped his fist in the air. Ty's teammates poured onto the field to greet him as he crossed home plate.

With one exception. Junior Bennett spat on the ground, threw his glove across the dugout, and stomped off toward the locker room.